P9-CDI-023

The Peculiar Incident on Shady Street

The Peculiar Incident on Shady Street

Lindsay Currie

Aladdin New York London Toronto Sydney New Delhi

ALADDIN
An imprint of Simon & Schuster Children's Publishing Division
1230 Avenue of the Americas, New York, New York 10020
First Aladdin hardcover edition October 2017

For information about special discounts for bulk purchases, please contact Simon & Schuster Special Sales at 1-866-506-1949 or business@simonandschuster.com.
The Simon & Schuster Speakers Bureau can bring authors to your live event.
For more information or to book an event contact the Simon & Schuster Speakers Bureau at 1-866-248-3049 or visit our website at www.simonspeakers.com.
Jacket designed by Jessica Handelman
Interior designed by Mike Rosamilia
The text of this book was set in Centaur MT Std.
Manufactured in the United States of America 1217 FFG
4 6 8 10 9 7 5 3
Library of Congress Cataloging-in-Publication Data
Names: Currie, Lindsay, author.
Title: The peculiar incident on Shady Street / by Lindsay Currie.
Description: First Aladdin hardcover edition. | New York : Aladdin, 2017. |
Summary: When lights start flickering and temperatures suddenly drop, twelve-year-old Tessa Woodward, sensing her new house may be haunted, recruits some new friends to help her unravel the mystery of who or what is trying to communicate with her and why.
Identifiers: LCCN 2016055681|
ISBN 9781481477048 (hardcover) | ISBN 9781481477062 (eBook)
Subjects: | CYAC: Haunted houses—Fiction. | Ghosts—Fiction |
Friendship—Fiction. | Mystery and detective stories. |
BISAC: JUVENILE FICTION / Horror & Ghost Stories. |
JUVENILE FICTION / Mysteries & Detective Stories. |
JUVENILE FICTION / Social Issues / Friendship.
Classification: LCC PZ7.C9354 Pe 2017 |
DDC [Fic]—dc23
LC record available at https://lccn.loc.gov/2016055681

For the creators of their own destinies.
May your adventure jars always be full.

1

Hi Rachel,

I can't believe they're making me do this. We're in the van already and it isn't even light outside. I begged them to change their minds, but they said Dad's new job is important to him and that families should support each other—not make each other give up the things they love. I don't even think they're listening to themselves or they wouldn't have made me give up Florida. And you. I miss you already.

Love,

Tessa

Rain batters the windshield of our ancient minivan, the wipers furiously working to keep the glass clear.

City lights fade to a blur in my tired eyes. We left Fort Myers on Thursday morning. Nineteen hours in a seat belt, four Twinkies, twenty-one old episodes of *The Simpsons,* and one cramped hotel later we finally get here . . . Chicago. The Windy City.

My parents keep saying this place is going to be everything we ever needed but didn't know existed. Whatever that means.

"Our house was built in the late eighteen hundreds, you know. So of course there will be some work to do," Dad says, loud enough so I can hear, but quiet enough not to wake my little brother, Jonah.

Mom is nodding enthusiastically. "I know. But it's so worth it. Think of all that original wood! And those high ceilings! It's a dream."

I roll my eyes. It *isn't* a dream, but there's no telling them that.

The car swerves violently around something in the road, and I crane my neck to see what it was. Shadows dance in the darkness stretched out in front of us. "What was that?"

"Just a limb in the road. Everything's fine. We're allllmost there," Dad says in that voice he uses when he's trying to lighten the mood. "You okay back there, honey?"

I look up but can't see his expression in the rearview

mirror. I'm kinda glad. If I could see it, he'd probably look wild and excited like he always does when he talks about moving here. About his new job.

Given that I just left behind my best friend, Rachel, a seventh-grade year that was going to be amazing, and my favorite drawing class, I'm not too interested in seeing that look right now.

"I'm fine. Just a little nervous. We're going to get there okay, right?" I ask as another small branch pings off our hood. Leaves are pinwheeling frantically through the air and landing on our windshield in a disgusting, wet mess.

"Of course we are, Tess. This is just a fall thunderstorm," Dad answers, leaning forward even more. "Nothing like hurricane season back in Florida. Remember all the times we almost evacuated?"

I nod but stay silent. Truth is, we did *almost* evacuate a lot, but we never actually had to. It was warm there, too. Like the sun followed you around just to kiss the tops of your shoulders and lighten your hair. Based on the few times we've visited here to house-hunt, I know it feels different. Colder.

Mom reaches back, looking for me in the darkness. I grab her hand even though I still feel angry. Deep down I know it isn't her fault. It isn't anyone's. When the Chicago Symphony Orchestra comes calling with an opportunity, you answer. And my dad—the best violinist in all of Florida—was the guy they called to audition when the first chair opened up.

I glance at Jonah, who is still sound asleep in his car seat. Both of his arms are wound tightly around Reno, the wooden ventriloquist dummy he refuses to go anywhere without. I hate the way Reno looks at me. Like he's watching me. Beady eyes, circus clothes, and a shock of black hair glued to wood . . . ugh.

Jonah settles deeper into his car seat and lets out a soft moan. I have no idea how he's sleeping through this disaster, but for a minute, I wish he weren't. Maybe if he started crying, Dad would stop the van. Maybe if he threw up, we could at least slow down a little. Maybe, maybe, maybe.

Dad sighs. "It's taken us an hour since we hit the city limits, but according to my GPS, the house is just around this corner. This looks familiar, right, Lily?"

"Well, it obviously looks different in the dark, but I think so," Mom answers, a nervous laugh escaping her lips. Mom is the most positive person I know, but I think she's just as scared about this move as me. Maybe even more.

I get it. I have no idea how she'll sell her paintings here or if she even can. There aren't any tiny seaside art shops or nautical boutiques here . . . and I can't imagine people in Chicago paying big money for pictures of seagulls and turtles and waves.

The car hugs the next curve as we turn slowly onto a narrow, one-way street. This is the right block. Small black wrought iron fences wrap around the trees. Parking signs jut up from the cement every few feet. A giant, metallic birdhouse-looking thingy sits on the corner. Mom says it's art, but I think it's horrible. Art is soft, and pastel, and shaded . . . *not* metallic and sharp.

"This is the right place," I pipe up, unable to keep the disappointment from leaking into my voice. I remember this block well enough from the two times we came to see the house. Mom and Dad drooled over it. I smiled when I felt like crying because although my parents are excited, I know they feel guilty for dragging Jonah and me here. I can see it in the looks they give each other when they think I'm not paying attention. I might miss Florida and all, but I don't want them to feel bad. *Life happens,* or so the bumper stickers say.

"Finally!" Dad breathes out. He pulls the car onto the small patch of cement they keep calling a driveway and turns it off. The headlights stay on for a few seconds longer, fixed on the wooden garage door at the bottom of the slope. I remember hearing that it leads into a parking spot in the basement. A drive-in basement.

So. Weird.

Dad twists around in his seat and squares his body off between Mom and me so he can talk to both of us. "Now remember, there's just the bare bones in here right now. A few things the previous owners left in here to make our transition easier until the moving vans arrive tomorrow."

Mom raises an eyebrow. "You mean, a few things that were too much of a hassle for them to move out. Right, Chris?"

Dad tosses her a wink and a grin in response. I squint through the rain, wondering exactly what was left in this place. Hopefully nothing gross.

Mom and I toss open our doors and make a run for it while Dad grabs Jonah from his car seat. I can hear my brother screeching from my spot on the front porch. The whole neighborhood probably thinks there's a wild animal on the loose.

Reno's knobby wooden knees clank together as Dad jogs through the gauzy sheets of rain. He sets Jonah down on the top step, then rakes a hand through his dripping-wet hair.

"Well," he says, fishing in his pocket for something. Hopefully the keys because it's freezing out here.

"Well," Mom echoes, taking a tearstained Jonah by the hand. He's clutching Reno like a life preserver. "This is it!"

Our new house is huge. Three floors and built like Fort Knox. Apparently Chicagoans call it a graystone, which is really just a fancy name for a cement house. I run a finger over the brick, shivering at how cold and unwavering it is.

Back in Florida, nothing was brick. Nothing was really this gray, either. We had houses that were blue, green, and even yellow.

I let my eyes settle on one of the second-floor windows. That room is mine. Mom picked it out during the house tour, started talking crazy fast about decorations and colors and how much I'd love the view. All I saw then was an old room with warped wooden floors and cracked paint. All I see now is ugly gray brick and the dark, gaping eye of a window. It's watching me, this house. Waiting to swallow me whole in its cobwebby corners and creaky closets.

2

I WRESTLE AROUND IN THE SCRATCHY SHEETS, wrinkled from too much time in a cardboard moving box. Light is streaming in through the window and I drape an arm over my eyes, shielding them. How can they sell a house without curtains? I mean, isn't that sort of like selling cake with no icing?

Sitting up, I lean over the edge of my bed and groan as two of my pastels come into view. The blue and the magenta. My favorite colors in the entire set are sitting on my floor, exactly where they shouldn't be. I glance at the open pastel box across the room. How did these colors get way over here?

I rub my bleary eyes and collect the pastels from the floor, vaguely remembering that I had a nightmare last night. There was howling out in the hallway. Or maybe it was crying. I'm not sure now, but just thinking about it makes all the hair on my arms prickle.

"Tess?" Mom's voice filters through my door as I snatch the pastels up, checking to make sure their fragile tips aren't broken.

"Yeah?"

"Breakfast is on the table. I have to go to the grocery store; we need actual food in here eventually," she says with a chuckle, and I clutch my grumbly stomach. We've been in this place almost two full days already and I haven't eaten anything that didn't come out of a bag.

"Okay. Dad's here, right?" I yell back, padding across the chilly wood floor to the sketchpad that's lying on my desk. Funny how all my clothes are still in boxes and not one permanent decoration is up, but all my art supplies have been unpacked.

I can't help it; I need them.

The door slides open a crack, and Mom's face peeks in. "Sorry, honey, I just didn't want to yell. I'm not up for waking Jonah yet."

I check the clock. Eight fifteen. "Why is Jonah still asleep? He's usually up at the butt-crack of dawn!"

Mom shoots me a dirty look, and I shrug an

apology. She's always hated that phrase, even though Dad and I think it's hilarious.

"He didn't sleep well last night. Honestly, I don't know what to call the dreams he was having . . . night terrors, I suppose." She looks thoughtful for a moment before continuing. "Such a brave boy for only four years old. I'm sure this move has been hard on him."

Night terrors. Poor guy. As annoying as he can be with that creepy little doll of his, I don't like to think of him having bad dreams. And night terrors sound worse than bad dreams.

"So, Dad's here and Jonah's in bed. Got it," I say, edging closer to my sketchpad.

Mom stares at me pointedly. "Tessa. You start seventh grade at your new school tomorrow. Don't you think you need to unpack bit more? Start settling in?" She folds her arms over her chest.

I have no interest in settling into this place. It's dark. It smells like old people and every single corner has a spider in it. No thank you.

"I will. I just need a few days." And a one-way ticket back home. I miss the sound of waves and the smell of the salt hanging in the air. I miss lizards and sand between my toes. I miss Rachel.

Rachel is the peanut butter to my jelly. The sour

cream to my onion. The sugar to my lemonade. She's my best friend, and I had to leave her behind. It's wrong. It's so, so wrong.

I reach up to my collarbone and rub the small silver locket between my fingers. It's the only thing connecting me to her now . . . the only thing we share. Rachel's is strung on black leather instead of a chain, and the picture inside is of me; otherwise they're identical.

Mom crosses the space between us and pulls me in for a hug. She smells like lavender. Tilting my chin up, she smiles and the little mole to the right of her mouth winks at me.

"This is going to get easier, honey. I promise. I'll make a space for myself to paint here, and you'll keep drawing. We're artists. Creators of our own destiny!"

Brushing the hair off my forehead, she kisses the top of my head. I wish I could believe all that, but I don't. Not when I have to walk through the doors of a completely new school tomorrow. Make new friends and find my way down new streets.

Mom pulls away, then hovers by my door for a minute. "There's beauty in this place, Tess. You just have to look for it."

"I'll try," I say, mostly because I trust her. Mom and I have always seen eye to eye on things, probably because we're both artists. She sees the world in sea-glass colors, and I love her for it.

The door clicks shut behind her, and I grab a pair of jeans off the chair I slung them over last night. My sketchpad is open just slightly and I stop in my tracks, confused at the small blur I can see in the upper left-hand corner of the sheet. It's grayish black, like I started something and then just barely ran the pad of my thumb over it.

"What in the—" I start, bending closer to the page.

I didn't draw anything last night. I was so tired from carrying boxes all over this ginormous place that I crawled into bed without even brushing my teeth.

I stare at the mark. It's small and shaped like an upside-down *L*. Lifting the book and giving the paper a tap, I watch as the unwelcome spot becomes dust again and drifts into the air. There will still be a darkened area there, but I'll camouflage it with shading later. Still. There's something about that mark that bothers me. Something off.

Shutting the pad, I pull open my desk drawer and drop it in. Mom and Dad bought me this desk specifically for art, and it has a drawer that's wider than most. It's deep, too, plenty deep enough to hold several boxes of pastels.

The vibrations of Dad's violin begin to ring through my walls, and I can't help but smile. Even though it brought us here and has ruined *everything* I was looking forward to, I still love that sound. It reminds me of sunset nights, of grouper on the grill, and of cold iced tea.

It reminds me of home.

3

THEY SAY THE FIRST STEP TO ANY GOOD PASTEL is to create a solid outline. But it's really not that easy. Drawing that first line is scary when the paper staring back up at you is so stark. So white and empty. It's hard to make that first stroke across it, no matter if it's light or dark, because you're always afraid of messing it up.

I would have agonized over drawing that stupid upside-down *L*. No way did I do it and forget. Besides, I don't even have a subject chosen to draw.

Flipping the light on in the bathroom, I scowl. I'm already on edge because of the mystery mark I found in my sketchpad this morning, and the idea of getting ready in this bathroom isn't helping. Somehow it looks darker than it did when I was brushing my teeth last night. Creepier. Dingy black-and-white tile dots the floor, and a chipped bathtub that stands on four feet is perched in the corner. There's only one sink instead of the double we had in Florida, and a murky brown line rings the inside of it.

How long has it been since someone cleaned this place?

"Yuck," I mutter, searching the empty room for a stack of towels. With my luck they aren't unpacked yet and I'll have to dry my face on my shirt. Mystery brown lines. No curtains. No towels. I feel like I'm on one of those reality shows where people try to survive the elements. *And in today's episode, Tessa Woodward will attempt to survive a nasty bathroom!*

I settle for cupping water in my hands and splashing it over my face, careful to keep my hair out of the sink and away from the brown line. Swiping off the extra drops with the palm of my hand, I look in the mirror. My cheeks are flushed and I definitely look more awake. Better than nothing.

I'm just turning around to head downstairs when the round bulbs above the vanity begin to hum. One at a time, they start to flicker on and off. On and off. On and off.

Weird. I remember Dad mentioning the leftover

furniture and the leak we have to get fixed under the kitchen sink, but I don't remember him saying anything about electrical problems in this place.

A deep crackling sound echoes off the bare walls and my arms break out in goose bumps. Within seconds, it's all around me, like it's somehow leaking into the room from an invisible crack. I turn a full circle to see if I can figure out where it's coming from, freezing in my tracks as all four of the lightbulbs go dim, leaving me in near-darkness.

Aaaand, that's my cue. I head for the door, grab the doorknob and turn, but nothing happens. It won't budge. As I scan the metal plate around the knob, my hand begins shaking. There's no lock on this door. So why won't it turn?

"Mom?" I shout through the door, gasping as the lights dim even further. It's dark enough that I can barely make out the shadow of my own hand in front of me as I wrench at the door, kicking and clawing at the warped wood in an attempt to free myself. The crackling gets louder, filling my ears with something that sounds like terrifying raw electricity.

"Mom!"

I finally slide down onto the floor and cover my ears. The sound is so loud that it feels like it's going through my skin and into my body. I blink at the darkness but see nothing. I'm not sure if I *want* to see something at this point.

A sharp pain catches me in the ribs. I scream and scamper away from the door and into the opposite corner of the bathroom. Whatever has trapped me in this bathroom is definitely attacking. The lights flip on and my mom's face appears. Her lips are moving, but I can't hear anything. Nothing but the crackling, that is.

She reaches out and gently removes my hands from my ears. The noise stops.

"Tessa? Oh, honey, what happened?" she says, pulling me in close. I feel her arms wrapping around me and lay my head against her chest, telling myself to calm down and stop being such a baby. "Did I hit you when I opened the door?"

"The lights," I sputter out. "They were flickering and there was this sound—"

"Those lights?" Mom asks, cutting me off. She's pointing to the bulbs over the sink.

I nod. "Yeah, they almost went all the way out. All four of them! And the noise was loud—like a hissing and crackling sound." I look around at the walls but see nothing other than uneven color and a mess of cracked paint. No gaping holes where crackling creatures tried to force their way in. "I don't know where it was coming from, though."

Mom untangles herself from me and stands. She looks at the light switch and then down at me. Holding out a hand, she helps me to my feet. "I'm no expert on old houses, but I think there might be a simple explanation for both of those things."

I tilt my head at her, curious. "What?"

She gestures to the light switch. "See how the switch is halfway between on and off? I'm willing to bet that these Victorian houses have some pretty finicky electrical systems and maybe that was what caused all the flickering lights."

I stare at the light switch. It *is* frozen between the on and off position. "Did I almost burn down the house or something? I mean, the sound was really scary."

Mom laughs, a quiet sort of giggle that warms my heart. "Nah. I don't think you did any damage at all. Just scared yourself a little."

Exhaling a shaky breath, I try for a smile. I know it's weak, but it's all I've got. I'm about to walk out when I remember the doorknob. Finicky electrical systems can't explain that. Are the doors really so old in this house that they don't open properly?

"The door was stuck, too. That's why I was calling for you."

She looks confused. Her bright eyes linger on me for a moment longer than usual before she shrugs.

“I didn’t hear you calling me. Honestly, it was pure coincidence that I walked in here. I needed to brush my teeth.” She lifts up her left hand to reveal the cosmetic bag she’s holding.

“You didn’t hear *anything*?” I say, stunned. “Not the loud sounds or me screaming? Nothing?”

Mom shakes her head. “I’m sorry, sweetie. The real estate agent said no one builds houses like these anymore because the materials were too good. Too expensive.” She knocks on the door as proof. “Hear that? This is a solid wooden door. Not hollow. Everything is just thicker than in newer constructions.”

Remind me that if I’m ever going to fall down or hit my head or pass out, I should try to do it in a room with an open door. Jeez. I turn back and face the mirror. All the pink has drained from my face, leaving behind an ashen-white mask.

“You going to be okay?” Mom puts her hands on my shoulders and gives a squeeze.

Nodding, I try to shake off the fear. I am okay. If I could survive the trip and the first day here, I can survive this creepy old bathroom.

4

MY LEGS ARE STILL SHAKY AS I WALK DOWN the creaky stairs toward the kitchen. Not a good way to start my second full day in this new place. Prehistoric, dust-covered furniture. Strange sounds in the night and now, possessed electrical systems. This house is starting to really bother me.

I pause to inspect a small painting on the wall—another one of the little things the previous owner left. It's not very big—maybe the size of a normal sheet of notebook paper—and based on the cracks in the thick layers of color, I think it's an oil painting. A simple, chipped tack is holding the top edge in place.

"Why would they just leave this here?" I ask myself, leaning closer. Mom leaves her art places sometimes, just to surprise someone who might not otherwise have money for "luxury purchases," but I don't. I don't want anyone else seeing my drawings. Not yet.

I squint in the dim light, cursing the bare bulb hanging over my head. The image looks almost like a garden, with long tendrils of flowers winding up a high stone fence. It's kind of creepy, nothing but a wall and those bright red petals, but at the same time it's beautiful. Good contrast, as my art teacher would say.

Swallowing hard, I tell myself not to think about my art teacher, Jane. She was short and blond and had the highest-pitched voice I'd ever heard. And she was also *amazing* at pastel drawing. My throat tightens with the threat of tears, and I shake my head, hoping maybe the memories will just fall out permanently. At least then they wouldn't hurt so bad.

"Good morning!" Dad says, gently laying down his violin as I cross into the kitchen. Jonah is up now and grinning like a maniac. Syrup dribbles from his chin, and half a dozen McDonald's containers are strewn around the table. "Did you sleep well?"

"Ahh, yeah. I guess so. Had some weird dreams."

"Me too," Jonah says with a frown. "There were ghosts in the hallway."

I stifle a laugh. Thanks to Mom and Dad's laid-back

parenting style, Jonah gets away with way more than any four-year-old should. Including watching all those crazy staged ghost-hunter shows on the Travel Channel. Dad says Jonah is a man after his own heart. Mom says he's a free spirit. I say he's one bizarre little boy.

"There *were* ghosts!" Jonah insists, stuffing another spongy bit of pancake into his mouth.

"Okay, okay. That's enough, J. Let's focus on good things today, huh?" Dad says, pulling Jonah up into his lap. "We're in a new city, and it's beautiful out!"

My eyes track his gaze to the window. I don't see anything but clouds in the sky. It's gray out, just like this building.

"So, your first Sunday in the big city. Once we get settled in, we'll resume our normal Sunday family days, but your mother and I both have about a million forms to fill out and companies to call. So . . . the world is your oyster today! Whatcha gonna do?" Dad asks, a broad smile stretching across his face. There's stubble on his chin and bags under his eyes, but he looks happy.

I shrug. I want to be happy with him. I *really* do. Dad is awesome and I know how hard he's worked for this. Mom, too. But right now nothing sounds better than crawling back into bed, burying myself under the covers, and pretending none of this ever happened.

"C'mon, Tess. Chicago is filled with history. And beautiful spots for drawing." Dad pauses and glances over at the counter, at an old Mason jar sitting on it.

I watch in horror as he crosses the room and grabs it, then brings it to me. With a clunk he places it on the table, leaving me to stare at the folded paper squares inside it. Dread fills me.

The adventure jar. Mom and Dad came up with this idea two years ago. They both write up "adventures" on little slips of paper and drop them into the jar, then wait for the perfect moment to spring them on either Jonah or me. Usually me.

"I don't feel like using the adventure jar, Dad," I mutter weakly.

"Nonsense!" Dad laughs as he lifts the jar and shakes it to mix up the papers inside before setting it back down. "This jar has been the catalyst for many a Woodward adventure! Remember that time we used the adventure jar and decided to just head over to the Keys for the weekend?"

Oh, I remember, all right. "Yeah, I missed a sleepover that weekend because no one checked the schedule before we left."

Dad snorts. "There's a sleepover every weekend,

Tessa, but the chance to see something new doesn't come along that often. You had so much fun in the Keys. Jonah, too. Remember all the amazing things we saw? And that was because we didn't sit around talking *someday* like most people do. We just did it." He nudges the jar toward me.

Sighing, I take it from his hands and begin unscrewing the top. I know Mom and Dad are trying to teach Jonah and me to be what they call "students of the world," and that I should appreciate it, but some days a girl just wants to sit on the couch and zone out. Apparently, that day is not today.

I cringe as I pull out a slip of paper. I was really hoping for an adventure that Mom came up with . . . something simple about finding one's inner peace, or whatever. That would at least have earned me some private time to chill. But there's no way that's going to happen now.

"'Explore the unknown,'" I say, balling the paper up into a wad in my palm and chucking it onto the table.

Dad's face lights up like he just won the lottery. "Wonderful! There are tons of opportunities! If you think about it, moving to Chicago is really just one big adventure."

"I'd rather have stayed in Florida, where I could be

sitting on the beach right now." I stare back out the window, my eyes landing on the gray sky.

His face falls slightly. "Hey, I know the first few days are going to be rough. They will be for your mom and me, too. But think of it this way—you can't see the world or all the wonderful things it has to offer if you keep your eyes closed."

My eyes are wide open; that's the problem, I think.

"Remember the place the real estate agent told us about? North Pond? That could be a perfect spot for you to explore today!"

I look at him like he's got three eyeballs. "I don't know where I am, Dad. I don't even know the name of our street. How am I supposed to get to North Pond?"

"Chicago is set up on a grid system, honey. If you know the coordinates of where you're at and where you're going, you'll get there."

I mash my lips together to keep from speaking. I don't want to wander around a strange neighborhood by myself. I'm not afraid or anything, I just don't want to. Not yet.

"Oh, and Shady," Dad adds, forking a bite of sausage into his mouth. He lifts the greasy napkin from the table and dabs at the corner of his lips.

"What?"

"We live on Shady Street. Literally just a few blocks

away from the pond. I wouldn't suggest it if it were dangerous; you know that. You'll be fine, sweetie."

A bubble of laughter slips out. "*Shady?* Our street is called Shady Street?"

Dad's eyebrows jump like he's confused. "Yes. Why?"

Shaking my head, I pull my sweater tighter. "Nothing, I guess. It's just . . . I don't know . . . ironic. The houses here are almost all gray, the art on the corner looks like a torture device, *and* it has barely stopped raining since we got here."

Dad wipes a blob of syrup off the counter. When he turns back to face me, he's smiling. "Ah. I see. You think *Shady Street* sounds sketchy. Well, Ms. Woodward, I think perhaps you're looking at this the wrong way. *Shady* makes *me* think of lying on a hammock under a palm tree listening to Jimmy Buffett."

I still think Shady Street sounds like it belongs in an R. L. Stine book or something, but maybe Dad is right. Maybe I'm not giving this place a chance. "Fair enough. But there's only one problem with your plan for me today. It's cold out."

"The ghosts were cold," Jonah interrupts, and Dad gives him a serious look. Jonah's small forehead wrinkles up. "They were! I promise! I was sleeping in my bed when they made everything like winter!"

Dad ruffles his hair and refocuses on me, but something dark is stirring in my gut. I can't quite shake off Jonah's words—*the ghosts were cold.*

I remember now! The crying woke me up in the night just long enough to realize that my toes were sticking out of the too-small quilt I've been using because my own bedding isn't unpacked yet. They were cold. Ice-cold. And so was everything else. I sat up to pull the quilt down over them again, and I'm almost positive I could see my breath. My breath!

That makes no sense.

"Dad, do you think there's something wrong with the . . . the, um, whatever the heat thingies are called in this place?" We never really needed heat back in Florida . . . especially not large, hissing metal boxes like these.

"The radiators? No, no, I think they're working fine. Besides, it's not even that cold out right now." He taps the face of his cell phone. "Yeah, it's fifty-three outside, Tessa. It probably just feels colder to us because we're used to Fort Myers weather."

Listening carefully, I hear the low *pssssst* of air coming from the box in the corner. The radiator. It's warm in here now, so he must be right.

"And as for the ghosts, I think our little man here has an unbelievable imagination. Going to make himself a fine artist or maybe even an author someday." Dad squeezes Jonah and they both laugh.

I stare out the window, taking some small sliver of comfort in the fact that Dad and Jonah seem happy. Why wouldn't they, though? Dad got his dream job and Jonah is just a baby. It isn't as hard to leave everything behind when you're not even in kindergarten yet. When I was in kindergarten, my goal in life was to learn to count from one to one hundred.

Dad snaps his fingers in the air, pulling my attention from the bank of clouds rolling past outside. "Go! Enjoy the leaves and the smell of wood fireplaces! Enjoy October! Before you know it, it will be November, and I've heard crazy things about winter in the Midwest."

Of course he has. Everyone has. Last year my science teacher said Chicago once had a polar vortex that killed most of the fish in every pond, lake, and stream in a nearly five-hundred-mile radius. And what did my family do? We came running here.

"Listen, your mom will be home soon, and I need to go down to Symphony Center for a bit. Maybe you'd rather come with me? Check out my new 'office'?" He says *office* with a smile, and I feel the joy radiating off him. I know he's excited and maybe I should be, too.

Still. It hurts. I don't want to see Symphony Center because right now, I hate it.

Jonah is clacking Reno's mouth in my direction, mumbling something I can't quite make out. The dark lines running down either side of Reno's chin are really just cracks that allow the mouth to move, but they look like blood. Black blood. I watch the rectangular pieces of wood as they click together furiously, mouthing out something . . .

"Wanna play, Tess?"

Hearing the words in Jonah's tiny, childish voice and seeing them synched up to Reno's mouth is unsettling.

I jump out of my chair and make a beeline toward the door. I can feel Reno watching me the entire way, sending a chill up my spine. I can never tell Jonah because it would hurt his feelings, but I don't just think Reno is ugly . . . I'm kinda afraid of him. Dad found him at a yard sale back in Fort Myers and bought him for five bucks—which I think was robbery for that thing. It belongs in some kind of spooky artifact museum, not in our house.

"No thanks. I think I'm going to take your advice and get out of here for a while." *I won't be gone long, and I won't go too far.* I silently add that last part for myself. Dad wouldn't care if I hopped a bus to the next town.

5

Hi Rachel,

Chicago sucks and I miss you. It's cold here and it rains SO much. Have you started school yet? I have to start tomorrow and I don't know how I'm going to do it without you. I'm still wearing my locket. Write me back!

Love,

Tessa

P.S. We aren't getting a house phone, but we will have Internet hooked up soon so I can e-mail you. Finally.

I tuck the letter to Rachel and my pastels into my messenger bag and then take my first steps down Shady Street. I know I should be unpacking, and right now I'd actually rather do that, but I also know Dad. He won't drop it until I've explored *something,* even if it is just the park in the middle of our cluttered new neighborhood.

North Pond is just southeast of our house. Dad showed me on a map before I walked out. I have a compass with me, one my parents bought for me two years ago when we were in our camping phase. All that connecting with nature was fun . . . when we didn't get lost or poured on. Mom doesn't like to obsess over the weather forecast, says you can stick your hand out the window and see for yourself. That might be true, but having a smartphone would make things easier. If I could use GPS to get to the pond, my phone would shout out the directions. I'd be there in no time! Instead I'll be trying not to fall on my face as I wobble through this strange neighborhood, completely focused on a tiny plastic bubble so I don't get lost.

I stop to wrap my sweater tighter around me as the wind picks up, looking down to make sure I'm keeping the needle of my compass tipped between the *S* and the *E*. The air smells gross, kind of like a combination of hot dogs and bathrooms.

"It's the sewer," Dad said as we caught a whiff of that same sour smell while we unloaded boxes from the moving truck. "Chicago's sewer system still has a lot of old clay pipes in it, and they're fragile. The constant construction causes leaks in them from time to time."

"The sewer?" I asked, wrinkling my nose as I grabbed another box. "Gross. How do you know that?"

Mom wiped a bead of sweat off her forehead and sighed. "Your father and I did a lot of research before deciding to move you kids here. A few odd smells here and there aren't enough to keep us from following your father's dream."

I stewed inside at that. What about my dreams? What about the school play and the art club I was planning to start? What about my first school dance—the one Rachel and I were going to attend together?

Something ahead catches my eye, and I shake off my thoughts. There's a clearing, a cluster of trees so beautiful it takes my breath away. Bright oranges and reds light up the cloudy sky like another planet shimmering off in the distance. I continue toward them, the first rays of hope welling inside me. The air smells cleaner suddenly . . . crisp and a little sweet, like fresh sketchpad paper. I like it.

Crossing one final street, I find myself standing in

the most gorgeous stretch of grass and trees I've ever seen. No buildings. No car horns or muffler exhaust. No ugly sidewalk artwork. Just color. Orange, red, and even a few bright yellow trees line the walking paths. I've never experienced autumn in the Midwest before, but I've seen pictures and this . . . this is it. As much as I hate the chill in the air, the leaves sure are beautiful.

A soccer ball lands at my feet. A boy who looks like he's about my age skids to a stop just in time to avoid crashing into me. He swipes his messy blond hair out of his eyes and smiles.

"Sorry. That one got past me." Dirt covers the entire front of the long-sleeved T-shirt and track pants he's wearing. A few splotches of mud speckle his tan skin. Except for his faintly nasal accent, he could almost fit in back in Florida.

I shrug and pick up the ball, then toss it back to him. "No biggie."

He grips the ball between his hands and looks me up and down. "You lost?"

Shaking my head, I try for a smile. "Nope. Just moved here, and I'm trying to find North Pond."

The boy's eyes light up, and I notice how blue they are. Like the ocean. "You found it. It's right over there." He points to our right, where I can see the light reflecting off something . . . presumably water. "Where'd you move from?"

A twinge of sadness needles me. I don't want to talk about Florida. I don't want to think about it, either.

"Far away. Like, it took us nineteen hours to drive here." It's all I can say with the choked-up feeling I have.

"Nineteen hours," the boy repeats thoughtfully. He taps his chin as if he's deliberating. "Gotta be somewhere like Boston or New Mexico."

I shake my head, a smile finding its way to my lips. "Nope and nope."

"Utah? Colorado? South Dakota!"

I laugh. He's firing off states so fast I can barely keep up. "Sorry, wrong direction."

He pushes an imaginary button, one eyebrow raised as if he's proud of himself. "Florida. My final answer is Florida."

Well, he nailed it. And suddenly the game isn't so fun anymore. "Yeah. Fort Myers, Florida." I exhale, reminding myself that it isn't his fault. He couldn't have known that guessing correctly would depress me.

He grins and pretends to pat himself on the back, then cranes his neck to look around me. "So you just got here and you've already ditched your parents?"

"They're busy unpacking and just wanted . . . well, they wanted me to get some fresh air."

"Ah. So you're one of those free-range kids, huh?" He looks at me expectantly, the edges of his mouth turned up into a half-smile.

Free-range kids? I wrack my brain for an idea of what this might be. Back home, we had athletes, mathletes, gamers, nerds, slackers, bullies, and everything in between. But I've never heard of a free-range kid. The term makes seventh graders sound suspiciously like poultry.

"Yeah, you know—that big movement to let kids walk around alone and be independent and all that. It's kinda weird, but kinda cool at the same time. I guess my parents are like half-and-half." He laughs loudly. "Half free-range and half 'you're grounded.'"

I giggle before I can stop myself. This guy is pretty funny.

Shrugging, I run the pad of my index finger over the outline of the house key under my sweater. "I guess I'm one hundred percent free range, then. My parents don't seem to worry about the things most parents do."

I force myself to stop speaking, shoot my brain a reminder that it would be an epic mistake to share my family's secrets. If I don't get control of myself, next thing you know, I'll be telling him about the adventure jar.

"Anyway, I should go. Have a good game," I add, turning to walk away.

"I'm Andrew. Andrew Martin," the boy calls out behind me. He's moving back toward the man he was playing soccer with, but his eyes are still on me. "Good luck in Chicago . . . um . . ."

I take a deep breath. Mom and Dad would want me to make friends here. Even if I'm never going to see this boy again, he's nice. I should be nice.

"Tessa. My name is Tessa."

6

AS IT TURNS OUT, NORTH POND IS PRETTY unbelievable. It's nothing like I ever imagined, with docks and wild grasses and even turtles! I've only been sitting here for ten minutes and already two families of ducks have swum by me.

Curled up on the very end of the dock, I breathe in the smell of the water and try to make myself believe I'm sitting in the sand on the beach again. I imagine that I have a sweet lemonade in my hand and my pastels all spread out on a beach blanket. If I didn't have goose bumps the size of raisins, I might believe it.

Running my hand over the collection of buttons on my messenger bag, I consider trying to draw. There are at least a dozen things I've seen here I'd love to draw, and since no one is expecting me home soon, I might as well try. The trees are perfect. The turtles are perfect. Even the water lapping against the posts of the dock I'm sitting on is perfect. I can't believe this place is in the middle of my neighborhood. It's like heaven.

I flip through my sketchpad to a clean sheet. My hand is shaking as I think about that first line. The line that always determines whether or not I need to erase. A cluster of lily pads in front of me would be the ideal subject . . . soft and hard at once. Deep green with the faintest hint of brown around the edges. Taking my colored pencil, a special Prismacolor one I use only for outlining, I shakily make the first of five small circles. Slowly. Steadily.

I'm about to finish the last circle when something cold and wet hits me in the nose. I wipe it off with the back of my hand and look up at the wall of gray overhead. *Great.* More rain. And I'm four blocks from home with no umbrella!

Does it ever do anything but rain in this place?

Quickly holding the sheet at arm's length, I look at the circles I just drew. They're good. Balanced and in the same pattern that the real ones in front of me are floating in. It's enough to work off, at least.

Snatching up my bag, I shove everything back in, careful not to crinkle the drawing I just started. Yet another reason I wish Mom and Dad would just let me have a cell phone. Then I could take a picture of the scene so I don't have to work only from memory.

Cold puddles splash under my feet as I sprint in the direction I think Shady Street is. Within a block, my sneakers are drenched and my toes are stiff with cold. Forget the cold. I need to focus on the compass. If I came southeast, I need to leave northwest . . . right?

By the time my house comes into view, my clothes are soaked through and my spirits are trampled. I'm afraid my new drawing is wet. Actually, I'm afraid the entire sketchpad might be. I fumble with the key Dad gave me, finally tossing open our front door and scrambling into the dry heat of our living room. Mom stands up from the box she's bent over, a mask of shock on her face.

"Tessa? What on earth is going on?"

"I got rained on," I say, swiping water from my forehead exaggeratedly.

"I can see that. But I thought you were upstairs unpacking." Mom's face is scrunched up into a bunch of worried lines and the color seems to be draining from it. "You . . . you were never upstairs?"

I shake my head. The way she's looking at me is

frightening, and I set my bag down on the floor. "Dad said I should go explore. He told me to visit North Pond." I say this so she knows I had permission to leave. Not that I need it. The adventure jar waits for no one.

Mom is shaking her head. Her eyes flick to the stairwell leading up to my room and then back to me. If I didn't know better, I'd think she was scared. But Mom doesn't get scared. . . .

"Mom? Is everything okay?" I ask.

She nods and the ghost of a smile lights up her pale face. "Sure. Sure, I'm positive it's fine. Probably just the wind or maybe a tree branch bumping around upstairs."

"You heard something? Like sounds coming from up there?" The hairs on my arms are standing up again, and this time the ones on the back of my neck join them. I haven't forgotten about what Jonah said—that ghosts were in the hallway last night. And I definitely haven't forgotten about the mark on my sketchpad. The mark I *didn't* make.

Mom reaches out to take Jonah's hand. He strains against her until she lets go, then makes a mad dash to grab Reno.

"C'mon, buddy. Let's go upstairs and make sure everything is okay in Tessa's room. Sound good?"

The noises were coming from my room?

"Ohh-kay," Reno's mouth clacks out. Jonah comes close to me with him and I scoot away, desperate not to be touched by any part of his spooky little wooden body.

The stairwell is still dark, and Mom groans. "Darn lightbulbs are all such a low wattage. We'll take care of those in time, though."

I stare at the picture on the wall as we pass. This time it looks even darker, more somber than it did earlier. The petals on the flowers seem almost . . . wilted. Strange. I remember bright red blooms on the flowers, not dark, wrinkled ones.

The same feeling I got when I saw the mystery mark in my sketchpad comes rushing back as I squint at the painting. Like something is wrong, but I have no clue what it is. How is it that this picture could look so different now than it did a few hours ago?

"Tessa, chop-chop. I have a lot of unpacking to do, sweetie."

"Sure. Sorry." I jog to meet them at the top of the steps, gasping as a cold blast of air hits me square in the face.

"Ghosts!" Jonah screams. Mom screams, too, jumping nearly a foot in the air at the sound of his voice.

"Jonah! Stop that! You scared Mommy." She brushes

a mop of brown curls away from his face and smiles gently, but I notice the hand that's still pressed to her chest. "You know even if there were ghosts, they wouldn't want to hurt us, right?"

I sigh. Most parents would tell their children ghosts do not exist. Not mine, though. They believe in letting us make our own decisions about things like that.

"There's no such thing as ghosts, Jonah," I say, but even as the words escape my lips I'm beginning to question them. Something about this place is just . . . off. The entire upstairs is freezing, so cold I can feel the icy air in my lungs when I inhale. Even with the rain it isn't that cold outside.

The lights flicker softly and then come back on full strength. Mom swivels her head behind her to look at Jonah and me. "Now, don't be nervous. It's just a storm. We've had more of those back in Florida than any of these Chicagoans."

Jonah looks at me, and in that moment, I see it. His fear. He honestly believes there is something upstairs with us, and I don't blame him.

I kneel down in front of him and try to make myself look as relaxed as I can. "It's okay, Jonah. I won't let anything happen to you. Mom, either. All right?"

He nods and pops a thumb in his mouth. Something

he hasn't done in about a year now. I stand upright and take a few steps toward my room, stopping when I notice the door is open a crack.

I shut that door when I left. I know this because I remember thinking it might stop Jonah from getting into my art supplies. Now it's open. And the air whooshing out is icy . . . not much warmer than the temperature inside our freezer.

Creeping slowly, I press on the door until it's standing fully open. And that's when I see them. My pastels. The blue and the magenta are sitting at the base of my bed again. Only this time, so is the sketchpad I put away this morning.

And it's open. . . .

7

SOMEONE ONCE TOLD ME THAT PART OF YOUR brain's job is to get your body ready to either fight or run when you're scared. I don't think my brain is working right because I have no clue what to do. All I know is that my heart is beating so fast I feel sick.

Something is really wrong in this place. I'm suddenly very grateful for the small reading lamp on my bedside table. It's not super-bright, but without it, we'd be in complete darkness.

"Are there ghosts in here?" Jonah asks, his bottom lip quivering with either fear or cold. I can't tell.

"Shhh. Not now," I answer him as I tell myself to stop being a chicken. Another cold blast of air hits me in the face and I notice that my window is wide open. The floor around it looks wet with rain. "How did that get open?" I ask no one, making a rush for it before the rain coming in damages anything.

I skid in the water, nearly falling as I struggle to pull the heavy frame closed. It slams down hard and I stand there frozen for a minute, hypnotized by the clouds that are quickly rolling in. They're turning the gray sky outside into a deep, boiling black. Like someone used a black pastel on a slate-gray page.

"Mom?" I call out, squeezing Jonah's hand in mine as I turn away from the window. Nothing. My heart pounds harder in my chest, so hard I'm afraid I'll be the first twelve-year-old to have a heart attack.

"I'm in the . . ." Mom's voice trails off and I hold my breath so I can listen for her. She sounds faraway, like she's in the walls or something. I put an ear to the peeling paint and listen. I don't even know all the rooms in this place yet and don't really want to go looking for her. Still, a part of me wants her in here.

"Mommy's hiding," Jonah says in a singsong voice, adjusting his hand in Reno's back. The doll's mouth moves slowly and his head turns to face me. It looks even scarier in the barely lit room. "Come out, come out, wherever you are!"

A rumble of thunder shakes the entire house and I scream. Lightning flashes outside, sending jagged shadows across my ceiling. *It's just a storm. It's just a storm. We had them in Florida,* I repeat to myself over and over again, desperate to make myself believe it.

"Jonah, stay right next to me," I say. "Until Mom comes back in here, I don't want you to wander off."

"I won't let Reno wander off, either," he responds. "He doesn't like the dark."

Me neither. I take a shaky breath and force my feet to move. Just another couple of steps and I'll be at the sketchpad and can see if there's anything in it. A message. A warning. *Anything.*

Lightning strikes somewhere outside and a loud crack vibrates around the room. This time Jonah starts crying, and I can't help him. I can't do anything except stare in horror at the open sketchpad lying in front of me.

The upside-down *L* is back, and this time, it's an entire rectangle. Four perfect right angles instead of one. The color is darker, too. It's an inky black with the hint of a shadow on the inside edges. Shadows are hard to draw. Really hard. This isn't just an accidental brush of a pastel against the sheet or some little bit of powder that got smeared on the paper. This is a real drawing. An intentional one.

I turn to look at Jonah, panic flip-flopping around inside me. I know it's crazy to think he could have done something as hard as this, but what other explanation is there?

"Did you do this?"

Jonah sniffles and stares at the paper. "Do what?"

Holding it up in front of my face, I point to the rectangle. Jonah hasn't messed with my art supplies in months. I can't figure out why he'd do it now. Besides, I've never seen him draw anything other than a stick figure. A perfectly shaded box? No way.

Stabbing a finger toward the paper, I try to breathe deeply and keep my voice calm. "This! Did you make this mark, Jonah? Tell me the truth."

"What's going on?" Mom appears in the doorway. She's wearing a heavy sweatshirt now, and her face is less pale than before. "I'm sorry, guys, the power cut out while I was digging through boxes in my room for something to cover up with. I had a tough time getting back here."

I swivel my head to the reading lamp. It was on the entire time. "The power? It didn't go out in here."

Mom laughs and waves me off. "Well, I don't know how that's possible. I was practically swimming through cardboard in the pitch black that whole time."

I blow out a confused sigh. If the power had gone out, wouldn't it have affected the whole house? In Florida we lost power all the time. Tropical storms and even the occasional hurricane warning would send us scurrying for our lanterns and flashlights every few months. But it was always the whole house—not just *some* rooms.

Mom runs a hand over my cheek. "Honey, are you okay? Did something happen?"

"I'm fine. It's just that you said you heard noises up here and there's this mark on my sketchpad."

Mom holds her hand out. "Can I see it?"

I nod and pass the sketchpad over, then watch as Jonah drops to all fours and begins peering under my bed. "What are you doing, J?"

"Looking for them," he whispers back, dragging Reno along with him as he crawls from the foot of my bed to the headboard. "Reno heard them up here, too!"

I rub at the goose bumps breaking out on my arms and try *not* to think about the noises or Jonah's doll being able to hear like a human. The only thing that really matters is the mystery box on my sketchpad. "You see it, right?" I ask hesitantly.

Mom breaks into a warm smile. "I do! What amazing right angles. And the shading is wonderful! What are you going to put inside the box?"

"I didn't make that," I say, watching her face for the reaction I know is coming.

Mom tips her head to the side, obviously confused. "What do you mean, you didn't make it?"

I shake my head and look around for any other signs that someone was in my room. Missing boxes, open drawers . . . anything. Why would someone break into our new house just to draw on my sketchpad? And how would they have gotten through without Mom seeing? My skin crawls with the idea of someone slipping around in the shadows of this house.

Running a finger over the edge of my sketchpad, I shrug. "I don't know how to explain it. But it wasn't me and I don't think it was Jonah, either."

She lifts Jonah from the floor, wedging Reno under her arm. His black eyes stare at me and I look away nervously. "Well, I suppose it could have happened during the move. Was the box you packed it in filled with pastels? Any open ones?"

I look at her quizzically. Mom might not draw the same way I do, but she's still an artist. She understands pastels and knows there is zero chance this was an accident. She's grasping for explanations. . . . She has to be.

"No. There were no open pastels and no boxes that combined the two things. And even if they were packed together, no accident could cause this kind of shading."

Just the thought is enough to terrify me. I sink down onto my bed and let my head drop into my hands. I don't look up until I feel the warmth of Mom's hand on my shoulder.

"Sweetie, we've had a long trip and your brain is tired. You should meditate tonight. Clear your worries!" She kisses me on the top of the head. "Who knows how this happened—maybe a friend of yours back in Florida thought that was a backup sketchpad or something."

I don't argue with her. I could tell her that Rachel knows me better than anyone and would *never* just draw in one of my good sketchpads. I could also tell her that as much as I love Rachel, she isn't into art. She'd rather be sweating on a soccer field than sitting in front of a clean sheet of paper any day.

But none of that really matters. It doesn't matter because the truth has clawed its way into my mind like the terrifying thing it is.

Our new house is haunted.

8

Hi Rachel,

Today is my first day of school and I'd kill to stay home. Actually, I take that back. I don't want to stay home. There's some weird stuff going on here. Scary weird. Sounds and flickering lights and things drawn into my sketchpad that I didn't draw. Wish you were here to help me figure it out. Anyway, I'll keep begging Mom and Dad for a phone because I'm dying to tell you all about it. Maybe it's Casper LOL!

Miss you.

Love,

Tessa

P.S. Do you believe in ghosts? Real ones?

The car rolls to a stop in front of Lincoln Park Elementary and I stare out the window at the swarm of students moving up the school's front steps. Like everything else, the building is brick and the steps are cement. This is exactly how I imagine prisons might look.

"When did you say the computer will be hooked up?" I ask. Part of me is stalling so I don't have to get out of the car yet, but the other part of me really wants to know. I miss Rachel. It would be awesome to e-mail her my notes instead of having them pile up in my bag like this.

"The computer is already hooked up, but it will be at least a few more days before we have Internet access. Why?" A flicker of concern crosses Dad's face. "Are you worried about getting your homework done? Because I can explain to your teachers if you—"

"No, it's not that," I say, trying for a smile I don't feel like giving. Still. I promised myself I'd try not to be so grumpy about all this—for Mom and Dad—and I'm going to do it even if it kills me. "I'll figure out the school stuff."

"Then what is it?"

"I miss Rachel."

The *glass is half full* smile Dad is always wearing

fades. He leans over and gently tucks a chunk of hair behind my ear. "I know you do, sweetie. And I'm sorry. Somewhere in all the chaos, I think your mother and I overlooked how hard that would be. Leaving your best friend."

I blink a few times, tell my eyes not to even *think* about watering. It's my fourth day in Chicago, my first day at a new school, and my best opportunity to make a good impression on the kids here. I can't do that with watery eyes and a splotchy face.

"You can use my phone any time you want," Dad continues, leaning over to pat my leg. "Call Rachel. I'm sure she'll be thrilled to hear from you!"

I'm sure she would, but I *hate* borrowing Dad's phone. Actually, I hate borrowing anyone's phone. It's frustrating to feel like someone is waiting on me every time I talk to Rachel. Plus, there're all the annoying chimes. E-mail, texts, calendar reminders . . . yeah, I need my own phone. Bad.

"This is a good school, honey. I really think you're going to like it here."

I nod as I watch a group of tiny kids racing toward the main door, lunch boxes in hand. They're squealing as they run and I can't help but think they sound like little sirens. Back in Fort Myers, I wouldn't even have been in school with kids their age. Middle school students had their own building, with only sixth through eighth graders in it. According to Mom and Dad, here the schools have kindergarten through eighth grade all in one school. *Huh.*

Dad taps an imaginary watch on his wrist. "Okay, kiddo. We've stalled enough. Get in there and have the best first day of school possible!"

He presses down on my seat belt latch to release it. I shimmy out of the belt, my eyes trailing a girl with a streak of blue nestled in her black hair. She stops by the car and slowly looks me up and down through the window. Blue Streak Girl doesn't look impressed.

I buckle my seat belt again. "I can't do this."

"Sure you can, Tess. You're a Woodward. You're strong and beautiful and . . ."

I hold a hand in the air, hoping he'll stop. I love my dad for trying to make me feel better, but I'm really just the new girl. One of probably two dozen who get stuck in this place every year.

Dad's face softens. "Listen, I know this is hard, and for the record, I owe you and Mom and Jonah a lot for doing it with me. Playing with this orchestra is a dream come true; kind of like if Mom got all those fancy art shops downtown to carry her paintings. It means a lot to me, honey, and I promise that once we get all settled in here, things will be great."

I clench my teeth together to keep from telling Dad what I really think. That his violin has just gotten us trapped in a real-life haunted mansion.

Dropping a hand to the door handle, I sneak a quick glance into the backseat. Jonah is sound asleep in his car seat again. Reno is sitting beside him, half slumped over. "Don't let him take that into school, Dad. He'll get made fun of."

Dad looks thoughtful for a moment, then chuckles. "I agree with you on that one. I'll keep Reno with me, tell Jonah I'm giving him a tour of Symphony Center while he's in preschool."

He leans over and hugs me, pulling back quickly and sticking both palms in the air. "Too much? Have I crossed the parental line that shall not be crossed on school grounds?"

I can't help but laugh. He has no idea how many hugs I could use right now. "It's okay, Dad. I'll see you after school. *If* I survive." Tossing open my door, I crawl out. Then I stay in that exact same spot and watch as he pulls away, waving the entire time.

I should go into the school. I should go get this

over with. Instead I find myself staring at a large sign in the front lawn that still reads WELCOME BACK TO SCHOOL even though summer break ended here almost a month ago. Guess they don't get around to changing their signs very often in Chicago.

"Hey! Florida!" A familiar voice breaks through the chatter of kids milling around me. It's the boy from North Pond—Andrew. He's wearing a plaid button-up shirt and a backward baseball cap.

"Hi," I say, grateful to see at least one familiar face. It's better than nothing, anyway.

He adjusts the backpack slung over his shoulder and smiles. The sun is hitting him just right for me to see the scattering of freckles across his nose. They kinda look like the Milky Way.

"I didn't know you were coming here. That's awesome. You're going to like it. Well, everything except for Mrs. Pollack, anyway. She's, ahhh . . . grumpy."

Laughing, I remember how much everyone disliked Mr. Leon, the natural environments teacher back at my old school. While most of our teachers were young and had a lot of energy, he was older. Crankier. He spent more time picking food out of his mustache than actually teaching, too. Rachel called him Mr. Peon, which I eventually figured out means she didn't think he was very smart.

I hike my bag up and look at the steps. They're emptying out; must be getting close to the first bell.

Andrew catches me looking in the direction of the front door. "So, um, do you have a schedule yet?"

"Yeah, somewhere." I dig into my jeans pocket and come up with a wrinkled slip of yellow paper. Andrew takes it from my hand and flattens it against the railing at the base of the steps.

"Do you know who any of those teachers are?" I ask, hoping his answer is yes. Planning ahead is kinda my thing and one of the characteristics that makes me so opposite my parents. While they prefer to "go where the wind blows us," I like to have an agenda.

Andrew smirks. "I know all of them. Why—you nervous, Surfer Girl?"

"Of course not," I lie. "And just because I'm from Florida doesn't mean I'm a surfer girl." The words sting a little coming out, like just imagining a gleaming-wet surfboard sitting in the sand is enough to make me homesick. I wasn't a surfer there, but right now I'd give anything to go back and try.

Andrew's eyebrows wrinkle together as if he can sense my sadness. "Hey, you're in my homeroom, so we can walk together." He folds the schedule into fourths and hands it back before picking up his backpack. "We better get going, though, or we'll be late."

I trail behind him, wondering who I've just aligned myself with. The athlete? The math geek? The slacker? Every school has them, but Andrew doesn't really seem like any of those.

He just seems nice.

9

I CURL MY TOES IN MY SNEAKERS AND STARE out into the sea of strange faces. I'm sure Mrs. Medina is going to be a fine teacher and all, but insisting that I get up in front of the class to "say a few words" about myself was a really rotten move. And on my first day!

Andrew gives me a small nod from the corner. I try to smile back, but I'm too nervous.

"My name is Tessa Woodward. I . . . uh . . . I just moved here from Florida."

Say something about myself? Done and done. I start heading back to my chair, freezing in my tracks as the teacher holds up a hand to stop me.

"I'm sure there's more to know about you than

that, Tessa!" She smiles warmly. "Tell us more! Do you play any sports?"

Slinking back into the center of the room, I shake my head. "No sports."

"Instruments?"

"No."

"Dance?"

"Ahhh, no." I almost laugh at this. I'm the most uncoordinated person on the face of the earth. One time Rachel tried to teach me how to slow dance and after the fifth time I stepped on her, she said if she didn't quit right then, she'd end up with a broken foot.

"Anything else you'd like to share?" Mrs. Medina asks, her once-warm smile growing strained. The silence in the room is peppered with noticeable giggles. Blue Streak Girl scours me with her eyes.

My cheeks flush. If I don't do something fast, my whole *make a good impression* chance is going to go down the drain. They probably already think I'm boring! Maybe I should tell them I paint, or that my mother received dozens of awards for her art back home. That's interesting, right?

No. I need to stick to the plan. Sharing anything too personal on my first day is a bad idea. I'll let the dust settle and figure out who's who before I say anything risky.

Think, Tessa. Don't get labeled as a big ol' yawn-fest.

"I live on Shady Street now. It's really different from where I used to live because it's super-old and all." My nerves are getting the better of me, making me jittery and tense, and it's taking all my effort not to run back to my chair, whether or not Mrs. Medina wants me to. The way she's looking at me is awful, like I'm under a microscope.

Students are shifting in their seats, shooting each other looks I'd recognize in any city. They're "the new girl is weird" looks, and if I'm not careful, I'll get them for the rest of my years here. I gotta give them something else. Something safe.

My heart beats faster and my hands go clammy. I really, *really* hate to improvise. The last time I was this nervous I completely lost control of my mouth and told my dentist about Rachel's crush on Warner Higgins. I even told him how she wrote *Rachel Higgins* on the inside cover of her history book because she was bored in class. I didn't mean to say it—I didn't mean to say *anything*—but I guess babbling is my specialty.

"I have a little brother—his name is Jonah," I blurt. "My dad moved us here because he took first chair in the Chicago Symphony Orchestra with his violin. My mom is an artist. A really good one. And Chicago is pretty good so far, except for the cold . . . and the smell . . . and the rain, and . . . my haunted house."

All the air is sucked out of the room in one giant whoosh. A few snickers break the silence, and Mrs. Medina shifts uncomfortably. Glancing over toward Andrew, I notice that instead of nodding or smiling at me like he did earlier, he's dropped his head into his hands.

Uh-oh.

The smell of stale peanut butter mingled with something like gym socks wafts past me and I groan, plunking a banana down on my tray. I'd give anything to be somewhere else right now. Anywhere but this smelly, loud cafeteria.

I close my eyes and imagine how great it would be to have a friend here. Just one friend. Andrew seems nice and all, but is he a friend? Maybe. *Hopefully.*

Letting my eyes flutter open, I notice that the girl with the blue streak in her hair is sitting by herself two tables away. Her mouth is downturned, and her pale face is pinched like she just bit down on a lemon. As if she can sense me watching her, the girl's eyes suddenly snap up to meet mine.

"Can I help you?" Blue Streak Girl asks.

Turning around to look behind me, I realize there's no one there. She's talking to me. I lift my brownish banana into the air. "Maybe. This banana *is* pretty hard to open."

I let out a weak laugh, hoping she'll stop looking at me like I just fell out of a spaceship. She doesn't. Instead, her eyes narrow into unfriendly slits. "Look, I know you're new and all, but the staring thing is getting old."

I don't know what to say. She's not wrong; I *have* been staring. It's just that I never realized how hard it would be to figure out brand-new people until I had to do it. I look back down at my tray, focus on opening my plastic silverware like it's a serious task. It keeps me from having to look directly at her again.

She lets out a long, tired-sounding sigh. "You're the girl who said she lives in a haunted house, right?"

"Maybe," I respond coolly, hoping she can't tell how upset I am. Doesn't matter that I'm tired and scared and miss Rachel so bad it hurts. I still shouldn't have said what I did. Haunted! Guess I have *two* things to work on now: staring and word vomiting.

"Hey! Where have you been hiding?" Andrew appears, setting his tray down. There's another boy with him, and a girl I haven't seen before, too. The boy has a look of amusement plastered on his face, but the girl seems anxious. Her huge brown eyes are darting around like fish in a bowl and she's gripping her backpack tight against her chest.

I start to answer Andrew's question but suddenly realize he isn't talking to me. He's talking to Blue Streak Girl. My mouth falls open, but I snap it closed before anyone notices.

They know each other?

"I haven't been hiding. Just . . . busy," she answers sharply. It doesn't sound angry exactly, mostly just guilty. Like maybe there's some truth to what Andrew is saying but she doesn't want to admit it.

"With what?" he presses.

"Stuff."

"Stuff," Andrew repeats flatly. "Since when do you have too much 'stuff' to go to a movie with us? Or to get gelato? Or—"

Blue Streak Girl holds a hand up in the air. "Okay, okay. I get it. *Jeez.* I'll be better."

Her words tumble out in a hushed tone. Andrew watches her skeptically. "If you say so. Because seriously, I have a hermit crab at home I see more than you lately."

With this, he pats the bench next to him for her to sit down. Wow. I struggle to keep the surprise out of my expression, but it's hard. Andrew and Blue Streak Girl don't just know each other.

They're *friends.*

10

"WHOA! YOU STILL HAVE JIMMY?" THE BOY who came in with Andrew exclaims, startling me. "That crab must be a hundred by now."

"Um, he's five," Andrew corrects. "And very proud to be on his seventh shell."

A hint of a smile plays on Blue Streak Girl's lips. I would laugh at the whole crab-named-Jimmy thing with them, but I can't. I'm too confused. So far, she's the only bad thing about this school—other than the food—and finding out that she's friends with Andrew is . . . I don't know . . . disappointing.

Andrew laughs and gestures to the friends who've taken up spots next to him. "Oh, Tessa—this is

Richie Whitfield and his sister, Nina. They live just down the street from me."

Richie gives me a quick nod before stuffing a handful of soggy fries into his mouth. Nina smiles shyly, barely making eye contact. Now that I look at them closely, I realize that even though they're not the same height—he's tall and she's short—their faces are similar. Same brown eyes, same brown hair—twins, maybe?

"Nice to meet you," I say. It *is* nice to meet them. I could use more friends in this place.

"And this is Cass Stone." Andrew gestures toward Blue Streak Girl.

Cass. I wonder if it's short for Cassidy, and then realize I shouldn't care. Mom would probably say her karma is terrible and that she's giving off negative vibes. I say she's flat-out rude.

"We met," she mumbles, barely taking her eyes off her tray. She reluctantly sets it down at our table and lowers herself to the seat.

O-kay.

"Tessa is new here. She's from Florida," Andrew continues. "I was thinking we could show her around and stuff. You know, educate her on which teachers allow gum in class and which ones don't."

"I'm in," Richie says. He tips to the side and bumps into his sister's shoulder. She wobbles, catching her balance just short of toppling off the end of the bench. Most girls would probably punch him or something, but she settles for a quiet glare. "Nina is in, too."

"Awesome." Andrew dramatically lifts a milk carton into the air. "I hereby proclaim this the beginning of Project Tessa. May she never embarrass herself in homeroom again!"

A deep belly laugh erupts from Richie. Nina takes a break from glowering at him long enough to smile around a mouthful of sandwich. Cass, though—she looks even more irritated than she did before. Wordlessly, she begins stacking uneaten food up on her tray.

I can't help it . . . I open my mouth again even though I know it's a bad idea. "Aren't you going to eat any of that?"

"No."

"Why?"

She straightens her hunched shoulders and looks me straight in the eyes. "Why do you care?"

Andrew's face falls. "Cassidy."

She shoots him a death glare. "Stay out of it, Andrew."

Sighing, he holds both palms up in the air as if he's surrendering. Maybe he is. She does look pretty frustrated.

"I didn't say I care. I'm just curious," I say. It's the truth. Something tells me Cass isn't as tough as she wants me to think. More than anything, she seems sad.

Cassidy stands up with a huff. Her tray is clutched in white-knuckled hands, and I notice for the first time that her arm is covered in multicolored silicone bracelets. They look way too cheerful to be on her wrist.

"Look, I'm late to meet Ms. Geist. I gotta go. Maybe I'll catch you guys later."

Andrew, Nina, and Richie mumble out their good-byes. Their eyes bounce around the table, silently questioning each other. Probably trying to figure out what's wrong with their friend.

Friend. I'm still not over it.

Cass shoves the contents of her tray into the trash and stalks away. Even though she didn't say it, it's obvious I'm the reason she's upset. So much for this day getting better. So far I'm enjoying it about as much as the nasty sewer smell on Shady Street.

I poke at my banana, wondering if Cassidy will hate me forever. I remember last year when two eighth-grade girls decided their life goal was to make Rachel miserable. Writing on her locker, tossing random food onto her tray at lunchtime, and giggling about her every chance they got . . . they were awful.

Fortunately, Rachel is the strongest person I know. I still smile when I think about the way she turned the tables on them. One day, her great-grandfather showed up at school and talked at an all-grades assembly about their family's Native American roots. He discussed local legends and even told some of the bedtime stories he'd heard as a child, growing up on a reservation.

Then he talked about the curses.

I swear he looked directly at those mean girls while he described the ancient curses, a tiny smirk hiding in his wrinkles as their eyes widened with each word. Of course he told everyone at the end it wasn't real, that the curses were nothing more than myths, but those two girls never bothered Rachel again. They never so much as looked at her.

She won. So can I. I reach up and touch the locket around my neck, telling myself I can be like Rachel if I need to be. I can survive this place. Sadness claws around in me as I run my fingers across the smooth metal. I miss her.

"Hey, don't let Cassidy bother you. She's . . . well,

I'm not sure what she is right now. She's moody, I guess."

Moody? More like murderous. That girl seemed out for blood.

"So she's not normally like that?" I press Andrew for more information. "Angry, I mean?"

He arches one blondish eyebrow at me. "No. Not at all. Cassidy has been our friend for a long time. Since second or third grade, actually. But something is up because lately she hasn't hung out with us as much."

"When?" I ask.

"When what?"

"When did she stop hanging out as much?"

Andrew looks thoughtful. "I don't really know. Guess I didn't pay attention. A few weeks ago, maybe? She just always had something else to do or somewhere else to be. So weird."

Even though it shouldn't, his comment makes me feel a little better. If Cassidy started acting weird a few weeks ago, it can't be *just* me that's bothering her. I wasn't even here yet! Though, based on the way she looked at me—like I'm a big fat mosquito buzzing around—I'm still part of the problem. I just don't know why.

I sink lower on the bench, feeling glum. It's then

that I notice it . . . the look on Richie's face. His eyes have skipped back across the cafeteria to where Cassidy is still standing. He gives her a look—something I can't quite read—and she rolls her eyes back at him. Richie just sighs and looks down at his tray.

What was that all about?

11

I'M STILL TRYING TO FIGURE OUT WHAT THE silent communication between Richie and Cassidy was when Andrew scoots closer to me on the bench, so close that I can smell the cheese sauce from his nachos. "So. About the haunted house."

"Nope. Not talking about this." I go to stand up but he puts a hand on my arm, dragging me back down. "Seriously, I shouldn't have said that. I was . . . I was just trying to be interesting. It isn't true."

"I saw your face, Tessa. You meant it. Your eyes were *huge*."

I'm opening my mouth to tell him he's wrong when I realize that would be lying.

Andrew's lip curls up into a satisfied smile. "You

can rule out a career in professional poker, FYI. You are a *terrible* liar."

"I know."

"So why are you trying to make me believe that you didn't mean any of that?"

I shrug and exhale. I don't really know the answer to this, other than to say that I'm afraid of what Andrew will think if I tell him the truth. That there's a mysterious box drawn in my sketchpad, my own bathroom went berzerko on me, and I'm scared every time I walk through the door of my new house. It makes me sound dramatic. Actually, it makes me sound like a lunatic.

"My mom used to think our house was haunted," Richie offers. "She said she heard all kinds of crazy things. It was scaring her."

I watch him carefully for any sign that he's baiting me—trying to get me to talk so he can make fun of me—but I see nothing. He looks serious.

"Yeah, that's happening in my place. What did you guys do?"

Richie guzzles the rest of his milk, then goes to open the second of three cartons on his tray. The guy must really like white milk. "We called an exterminator. Turned out there were rats in our walls. Big black ones with teeth so long and yellow my mom fainted when they showed her."

I wince and look back down at my tray. I'm not thrilled to hear about the yellow-fanged rats in his house, but it gives me hope. Maybe the noises Mom heard were just some kind of rodent. But that still doesn't explain the box drawn on my sketchpad . . . or the way the bathroom turned on me.

"I don't think the things happening my house can be explained by rats. Or bugs or birds or anything else that could get in and make noise." I pause, unsure of how much to actually share with them. "I do a little drawing . . . I mean, I'm kind of an artist. Whatever is making the noises in my house also drew something in my sketchpad."

Silence. A lone fry dangles from Richie's lips, and if it's possible, his mute sister's eyes open even wider. Andrew picks at the last of the nachos on his tray for a few long moments, then pushes it away and focuses on me.

"I knew I saw you drawing down by the water the other day. I wanted to come over and talk, but my dad had a work meeting so we had to leave." He pauses thoughtfully and then looks me in the eyes. "What did they draw?"

I think back to the perfect right angles and the unbelievable shading. Even now, it gives me goose bumps. "A box."

"Anything in it?" Ritchie asks, swapping his last white milk for his sister's chocolate. I haven't seen her eat a thing off her tray yet.

I shake my head. "Nope. It's empty. But there's this painting on the wall in my hallway that keeps changing, too. Like the colors get darker or the picture gets sadder or something."

I can't believe I'm telling them this.

"Where do you live again?" Andrew asks.

"Shady Street. Not far from the pond where I met you."

Andrew runs a hand through his shaggy hair, leaving it standing on end. "I live close to there. On Surf. Maybe we could come over sometime. Take a look around with you."

"Definitely. Thanks."

"This neighborhood used to be a graveyard." Nina's voice comes out of nowhere, startling me.

She finally said something!

Nina's huge eyes are focused on me now, like saucers of brown paint. If I had to classify them in pastel terms, I'd say they're cocoa bean. They remind me a little of sea oats, only a few shades darker.

"Seriously?" Ritchie asks. "How would you know that?"

"I read about it," Nina says matter-of-factly. The

shyness in her expression has disappeared and now she looks almost . . . excited. "Back in the eighteen hundreds, the people who were buried there started coming—well, they started coming back up."

"What?" I ask. "Coming back up?" The chill that digs into my body every time I think about my house is back.

"Ugh. God, again, Nina?" Richie moans. "Enough with all this paranormal crap."

Nina exchanges an annoyed glance with her brother before continuing. "The bodies were buried too close to the lakefront. The moisture in the soil started making the graves all loose and stuff, so the dead people kind of—"

"Kind of what?" Andrew interrupts. I can feel icy fingers along my spine and I have to force myself to stay seated. Truth is, I want to get up and walk out.

"They didn't stay buried for long. Let's put it that way. Most of the bodies were eventually dug up and taken to a graveyard up north. They're still there, if you want to go look sometime."

"Walk around a creepy old cemetery?" I ask her. "No thank you."

Andrew looks thoughtful but stays quiet. Richie has abandoned his fries and is looking at me intently. Like he's not sure whether or not he even wants to stay sitting at my table. Like maybe having a haunted house is contagious.

Nina shrugs and looks back down at her tray. Her long brown hair shifts like a curtain around her face, hiding her fishbowl eyes. Seeing her get so shy again makes me feel bad, but I *really* don't want to go wandering around a bunch of tombstones with her.

"Thanks for telling me all that, though. You never know, maybe one or two of those bodies didn't get relocated." I laugh nervously. The idea is nasty.

"Twelve thousand. Around twelve thousand bodies are still in the ground underneath the Lincoln Park neighborhood. Well, and parts of Gold Coast."

"Under my house?" I practically scream.

Nina shoots me a disturbingly serious look. "Under all of ours."

12

EVERY GOOD ARTIST DOES SOME RESEARCH BEFORE starting a big project. Two years ago, Mom painted for over four months on the same scene: a view of the harbor just down the road from our house. She went there almost every day, looked at it from all different angles and in lots of different light before deciding on one. Thanks to her research, the one image she chose to paint was perfect.

I'm beginning to think Nina has done some of the research I need to solve the mystery of what's happening in my new house. I just don't know why.

Andrew is jogging just ahead of me, waving back at me to hurry up. "C'mon, Tessa! Move it! The bell already rang."

Pulling the crumpled yellow schedule out of my pocket, I try to read it and watch where I'm going at the same time. Two crashes later, I realize it isn't possible. "You're in this class with me, too?"

"Yup. And last period. But if we don't get in there fast, Mrs. Abrams will lock the door."

Lock the door? Jeez. This lady must be really serious about—I take a quick glance down at my schedule—gym? "How can she be that insane over gym? Isn't it Ping-Pong and push-ups and wall ball?"

Andrew laughs. It's a great sound. "She's ex-military. At least that's the rumor. She came back from some assignment overseas and got a job here," he huffs out.

Pictures of a stern woman with a brush cut flash through my mind. I shake them off and refocus on trying to memorize the route we're taking. Eventually I'll have to be able to do this on my own.

The doors to the gym swing open and I breathe a little easier. It would be awful to get locked out of one of my classes on my very first day. Well, on any day, I suppose. I've never been a straight-A student, but I always do okay.

We're just about to go our separate ways—me to the girls' locker room and Andrew to the boys'—when I pull him to a stop beside me. "What's the deal with Nina? She seems nice and all, just a little—"

"Weird?" he offers up with a smile.

"Maybe a little. My best friend back in Florida knew a lot about Pokémon, but I've never known anyone who knew so much about graveyards before."

"Yeah, she's always been different. She and Richie are twins, but they've always been opposites. He's loud and she's quiet."

I think about this, remembering how her eyes went from nervous and shy to excited all at once. "Twins, huh? Weird."

Andrew shrugs. "Weird is right. I've never met any two people who're more different than them. Hard to imagine they shared the same stomach for nine months!"

I laugh at the thought. Richie was probably stretching out and taking up all the space in there while Nina was glaring at him. "I hope she didn't think I was being rude or mean or whatever. She just surprised me with all that stuff."

"Nah, she's fine. Probably was happy you didn't laugh at her."

"I hope you're right. Hey, um . . . I'm sorry about earlier. With Cassidy."

"What are you sorry about?" he asks, one hand on the doorknob of the locker room.

I sneak a glance at the freckles sprinkled across his

nose and cheeks. They aren't as obvious as they were when he was standing in the sun earlier, but they're still there. Still intergalactic.

"I don't know. It just seemed like I upset her somehow. Like maybe there's something about me she doesn't like."

"She doesn't even know you, Tessa."

"I know. But—"

Andrew shakes his head, cutting me off. "Don't. Cassidy is nice. I promise. I don't know why she's acting so strange, but I know it isn't about you."

If that's true, why does it feel like it is? I ask silently. The way Cassidy reacted to me in the cafeteria wasn't the way most people react to a new girl—a girl they don't know. It was the way my mom reacts to commercials for Chia Pets.

She was annoyed.

"Do you think she'll tell Richie? I mean, do you think she'll tell him what's bothering her?" I hold my breath, hoping for a clear yes. It's not like I'm obsessed with making Cassidy like me or anything, I just want things to be better here at school than they are at home. I've already got a haunted house to worry about; the last thing I need is a mean girl, too.

Andrew shrugs. "Maybe. They're pretty tight. Science nerds, you know?"

Science nerds. No, I do not know. And I'm confused. "What do you mean?"

"I mean they're both really into science. They're even in a club together after school. Meets once a week, I think."

Interesting. The thought makes me feel hopeful. If Richie and Cassidy are in a club together, there's definitely a chance that she'll confide in him. Tell him why she's so upset and if it's because of me.

"We better get changed. See ya after class?" Andrew asks hopefully, and I nod.

I'm beginning to think I wouldn't have made it through my first day without him. Or his freckles.

The front door swings open with a bang, revealing a neat row of boxes in our living room where an enormous pile used to be. I slide off my jacket and drop my backpack.

"So it wasn't too bad, then, huh?" Dad asks as he shuts the door and drops his car keys on the small round table. It's our junk table and came here with us from Florida. An artist friend of my mom's carved it out of driftwood years ago and we've used it ever since.

"It wasn't bad. Just . . . different," I say, remembering that the only bad part of my day was that Cassidy girl and my accidental haunted house outburst.

Dad throws an arm around me and tugs me to his side. "It will get better, Tess. Much better. Just give it time."

A loud crash in the kitchen breaks our attention and Dad takes off, leaving me behind. The moment he disappears through the door, a gust of chilly air shoots up the back of my shirt. I turn back and notice that the front door is standing wide open.

I peek into the hallway hesitantly. Empty. I watch the sidewalk through the front window for a second, bewildered. I know Dad shut and locked that door when we stepped in. I heard the giant dead bolt sliding into place. So why is it back open now?

"Tessa, can you come in here?" Dad calls from the other room. I lock the door and head in that direction, looking back two different times on my way to make sure it isn't open again.

It's starting. I can feel it.

The kitchen is bright and there are dozens of utensils lined up on the countertops. Spatulas, knives, and can openers gleam in the overhead lighting. Mom is on the floor, digging frantically through a box. Wild curls of hair are falling loose from the bun at the nape of her neck, and she's sweating.

"Oh, good . . . the more eyes the better. Tessa, have you seen my watercolors?" she asks, her tone hopeful.

I shake my head. "No. But why would they be in a kitchen box?"

"They shouldn't be," she breathes out, obviously tired and frustrated. "I'm looking here now because I've searched everywhere else. They were so expensive; I'm really worried they didn't make it!"

Dad puts an arm around her shoulder and smiles gently. "I'm sure they're here somewhere, Lily. We'll split up and look if we need to."

"Are you on a deadline?" I ask. There have been times when Mom has been "commissioned" to do a painting of something specific. It would be horrible if her supplies went missing before one of those deadlines.

Mom grips the edge of the island and pulls herself to her feet. Even under stress, she looks beautiful. Bright blue eyes, wild hair, and pink cheeks—she's the prettiest mom I know.

"Thank goodness, no. I wrapped up the projects for all my clients in Florida before I left." She does a tight one-eighty to look around the room one last time. "I'm sure they'll turn up."

I glance around the room, noting that there's still a sea of boxes. "You're positive they aren't in one of these?"

"Positive," she says, huffing a chunk of hair out

of her eyes. "Everything else is here. The brushes, the canvases. Even my backup brushes!" Mom lifts a scraggly-looking brush in the air and shakes her head. Her face is drawn tight with confusion.

I lift the flap of the nearest box and peer inside. This one is filled with Tupperware. Mom has *dozens* of watercolors—probably close to a hundred. I don't get how they just . . . disappeared.

"Well, they haven't vanished," Dad says confidently. "Moving is nuts. They probably just got put in another area of the house."

Yeah, like that rectangle just happened to get drawn in my sketchpad.

Jonah barrels into the room, Reno clutched in his sticky-looking fingers. "Can I have a juice box?"

"Hey there, dude!" Dad sweeps Jonah up into his arms, adjusting Reno so that he doesn't lose an eye to the dummy's wooden nose. "Have a good day?'

"Yes. But the ghosts took Mommy's art stuff," Jonah says.

Dad's face drops as he looks at Mom. Her eyes flutter closed just slightly and then reopen with a sad shake of her head. "He's been saying that all day."

"Did you hear noises again? Coming from my room?" I ask, my heart pounding. If something happened to my supplies, too, that's it. I'll walk back to Fort Myers if I have to.

Mom shakes her head. "I haven't heard or seen anything weird. But Jonah . . . he insists that there're ghosts. I don't want to stifle his creativity so I just let him. Think I'm handling that okay, Chris?"

"I do," Dad answers. "Telling him to stop will only make him say it more."

Or maybe it wouldn't. Maybe if Mom and Dad actually punished Jonah, he'd listen better. They could start by getting rid of Reno. . . .

"Oh, Tessa, I'm sorry. I've been so focused on me that I forgot to ask you how your day was," Mom says, swiping a sweaty strand of hair from her forehead.

"It was fine. Don't worry." I sidestep Jonah and Reno, making my way toward the stairwell. The coldness from the tile seeps through my socks and I pause for a moment, wondering how many bodies are resting under this street. Under this *exact* floor. *Too many,* I decide, and scurry off to my room.

13

MY TOES ARE COLD AGAIN. THE THOUGHT SETTLES into me like a splinter, the kind you can feel but can never quite see. Half awake, I sit up and scan the darkened room. Wind is rattling the ancient windowpanes, and gnarled shadows dance along the bare walls.

Historical. Grand. Elegant. I don't care what my parents call this house. . . . It's scary. I remember what Rachel said when I showed her the picture of it. She mashed her lips into a tight line and tried to stay positive, but it didn't take a genius to tell how she really felt. She thought it was old and run-down, too. And if Rachel thought that—if the girl who'd kept a smile on her face even when she got head lice in fourth grade wasn't positive—then it couldn't just be me.

I try not to think about what Nina said in the cafeteria yesterday—that this whole neighborhood is built on top of a graveyard. Just imagining the bodies being dug back up is terrifying. I can't imagine how scary it was when they tried to claw to the surface on their own.

Yanking at the too-small quilt, I stretch down to cover my ice-cube toes. I'm just settling back into my pillow when I hear it.

The crying.

It starts out soft, then builds to a deafening wail that seems to be coming from the hallway.

"Jonah?" I whisper into the darkness. "J, is that you?" Maybe he got confused and can't find Mom and Dad. Maybe he's sick. Maybe . . .

Muffled footsteps ring through the walls, surrounding me. They sound like boots, or something with heels. Definitely not Jonah's bare feet. I pull the quilt up to my chin, terror overpowering my need for warm toes.

Please, please go away.

I cover my ears to drown out the crying. It's not Jonah, that sound. It's higher-pitched, like a little girl. The footsteps stop outside my door, and my doorknob rattles. It shakes harder and harder until I can't contain my scream any longer. It bursts from my throat and I leap out of my bed, scrambling toward the window.

A low mumbling follows me and the cold rush of air is back. It lifts the back of my pajama top and tousles my hair.

"Graceland. Graceland. Graceland."

I stumble over a pile of boxes, falling to the floor as my legs get tangled up in the broken cardboard. Lightning flashes outside, brightening up the corner of my room and . . . Reno. His horrible wooden face is turned toward me and something wet is streaming down his pale cheeks.

Tears.

His mouth is moving, clicking out *"Graceland"* over and over again as the liquid streams down the wood in fat rivers. "No, no, no!" I scream as the room begins to spin around me and the familiar crackling slowly builds in my ears. A deep rumble of thunder echoes off the walls, the popping sound growing so loud that I can feel it. It's snaking through my veins like a dark energy. An energy I can't control . . . can't escape.

I'm going to faint. I'm going to faint and that horrible doll is going to do something to me.

Then everything goes black.

14

"TESSA? CAN YOU HEAR ME?" A VOICE DRIFTS past me somewhere in the darkness. I try to open my eyes, but they're too heavy. "Maybe we need to call an ambulance."

The word *ambulance* brings me around. I've always been afraid of those things. Their horrible screeching and blue and red lights that flicker through the streets. I've never been in one, but I figure they're pretty scary inside.

"I'm okay," I mumble. My lips are thick and making words with them is hard. I go to lift my head, but it won't move. "Just gimme a minute."

"She needs more than a minute. Lily, can you get her some water?" It's Dad's voice. I recognize it. Unfortunately, I also recognize that he sounds scared.

Something cold and wet sloshes over my forehead and I gasp. My eyes finally find the strength to open, revealing the bright red cheeks of my mother. "Oh, Tessa! Honey, are you okay?"

Okay? I'm not sure.

"What happened?" Dad asks. He's standing right next to Mom, but unlike hers, his cheeks aren't flushed. They're pale.

I lick my lips so I can peel them apart. What I saw in my room was so awful, so terrifying, I'm not even sure I can say the words. Just thinking them makes me shiver again.

I point to the corner, where Reno was sitting.

Mom, Dad, and Jonah all follow the invisible line my finger cuts through the air. "Reno? What are you doing in here?" Jonah scampers across the room and grabs the doll. Reno's mouth gapes open and his black eyes settle on me.

"No. Don't bring him over here!" I shout. "Look at him! Do you see the tears?"

Jonah lifts Reno higher and I watch as Mom and Dad inspect him. Mom looks back at me, her eyes wide and startled like a rabbit's. "What tears? Tessa, honey . . . I think you had a nightmare."

A nightmare? No. I wasn't asleep. I was wide awake and that doll was talking. My brain spins for a minute as I try to remember the rest of the details. The crying, the footsteps, and the door rattling. Then—*"Graceland."* I don't even know what it means, but I'm positive that's the word Reno was whispering. I shudder and pull my covers up to my eyes. I can't stop the tears from coming.

"Our new house is horrible. I hate it!"

Mom and Dad ease down onto my bed. Their faces are full of something I don't like. I think it's sadness. Maybe pity. I cry harder because I don't think they believe me.

"He *was* crying! I saw him! And there were footsteps and my doorknob was rattling!" I hiccup out through my sobs. I knew that doll was bad. I *knew* it.

"There, there. Relax, honey. It's going to be okay. No matter what happened, we're all here together now." Mom pats my leg, a smile barely brightening her pink face.

I force myself to look at Reno. The tears on his cheeks are gone now and his mouth is still. Closed. Reno always freaked me out in Florida, but he never came to life. Why now? Why in Chicago?

Suddenly, I have an idea. I sit upright and look at Jonah. "Did you hear it, Jonah?"

His messy brown hair is sticking straight up in the back and he's got a thumb in his mouth again. He just stares at me.

"Jonah, answer me! Did you hear the crying? And the whispering?"

I hold my breath as I wait for his reaction. He heard it. I'm positive he did. Jonah was the first one in this house to say there were ghosts—the first one to sense their presence. If Reno is somehow responsible for all this, surely Jonah heard him tonight, too. Right?

Mom smooths some hair off Jonah's forehead so his eyes are visible again. *Please say you heard it, too. Please say it isn't just me losing my mind in this place.*

Jonah looks straight at me and shakes his head.

15

I SPEND THE REST OF THE NIGHT CURLED UP on the oversized armchair in the corner of Mom and Dad's room. I'm too old to be crawling into bed with them and I know this, but I couldn't sleep in my own room. Not after all that.

As I roll over and pull the blanket up higher, Reno's shiny wooden face crops up in my mind. I quickly try to shove it out.

I open my eyes and look around, surprised to see how bright it is and that Mom and Dad's bed is empty. The covers are all pulled up tightly and the decorative pillows are in place. What time is it?

The clock that sits on the end table reads 9:45. I fly off the armchair, tossing the quilt to the floor.

Why didn't anyone wake me up? It's a school day! Half jogging, I brush my teeth and my hair at the same time. Then I race for a change of clothes and some shoes.

I'm just about to leave my room when I notice that the top drawer of my desk is open. Creeping toward it, I inhale sharply as I realize there's something drawn *inside* the rectangle now. Something dark and curvy.

The outline of a girl. If there's one thing I know how to do well with pastels, it's outline, and this outline is sharp and clear. Definitely not the work of a beginner. The girl is sitting on a chair and holding a long object . . . maybe a cane or a stick. There are distinct ruffles on her sleeves and her hair is wavy. A faint smile is etched into her innocent-looking face. Underneath the outline is one word: *Inez.*

I drop the sketchpad and rub my eyes. Last night I was certain Reno was the cause of all my problems, but now I'm not so sure. Who is Inez and what would she have to do with my brother's ventriloquist dummy?

The fear I've been feeling slowly trickles away, leaving behind something else as I look at the outline in front of me. Something I haven't felt yet in this new city. *Curiosity.* What if Inez is the one I heard crying?

What if the ghost is a little girl? Either way, I have to know who she is for sure. Then I need to figure out what she wants.

I smell waffles as I race down the stairs, taking two at a time. Mom is standing in the kitchen and Jonah is sitting at the table. His dark hair is hanging in his eyes and Reno is lying facedown on the table. Mom turns and her eyes are bright today. Happy. Must be nice.

"Good morning, Tessa. Are you feeling better?"

"Yeah. But why didn't you guys get me up for school? And why is Jonah still here?"

Mom uses a bright green rubber spatula to scrape eggs out of the pan on the stove and onto a plate. "Well, the whole house was up last night. We figured you kids would be tired this morning."

I *am* tired. But I'm also anxious. I want to get to school so I can tell Andrew and Nina about the new drawing. Plus, I haven't been here that long. I can't just go missing school for no reason.

"You guys can't let me sleep in, Mom. This is middle school—there's a lot of work I'll have to make up."

"Oh. Well, all right then. Did you want me to call your teacher and let her know why you weren't there this morning and that it isn't your fault?"

Taking a deep breath, I remind myself not to get angry. It's hard, though, especially on days when I feel like my family does everything backward. "No. Please don't call her; it won't help. But next time wake me up!"

I head toward the table, whirling around to face Mom again as another even more disturbing thought occurs to me. "Oh, and please don't take us on any crazy last-minute trips that will make me miss school like you and Dad did last year."

Mom looks crestfallen. She brushes a few curls of hair out of her eyes and smiles softly. "But that was Indonesia, sweetie. That was a once-in-a-lifetime opportunity!"

"I know. It was great, but I missed a week and a half of everything. Biology, math, Spanish . . . It took me forever to catch up. Andrew and Nina said the high schools are really hard to get into here and attendance is just as important as grades."

"You're at the beginning of your seventh-grade year, Tessa. You've got at least another year before you even need to start *thinking* about high school. And I'm sure the neighborhood one is lovely."

"No, it's not!" I say. "I learned that my first day here just from listening to the conversations in home-room. The schools aren't the same here as they were in Florida, Mom. We'll have to plan so I can get into a good one." I place extra emphasis on the word *plan* so she gets the hint.

She wrings the dish towel in her hands and stares at me. She opens her mouth a few times to speak but closes it again right away.

I blink back tears, unsure why I'm so fired up about this now. Mom and Dad have always marched to the beat of their own drum. Compared to some of the other stuff they've done, not waking me up this morning wasn't really that big of a deal. She was just trying to let me get some sleep.

It's just that it's one more thing that makes me feel like an outsider. *Different.* And I don't need any more of those than I already have.

Can't they see that?

I take a deep breath and prepare to say the words that are sitting on the tip of my tongue. "I'll never fit in here unless you do things the way normal parents do."

"Normal?" Mom asks. Her voice cracks a little and I know I've hurt her feelings. I swallow hard. I really didn't mean to.

"Never mind. Forget I said anything," I mumble. Taking a few steps toward the table, I pause by the mess of wooden arms and legs that make up Reno.

He's sprawled out strangely, and the way his joints are bent, they look broken. I reach a shaky hand out and touch the thick black hair on his head.

"Don't!" Jonah snaps, and I jump back. My heart hammers in my chest as he scoops Reno up and clutches him to his front. "Reno is still scared of you after last night!"

"Scared of me? Are you kidding, Jonah? I hate that creepy little—"

"Tessa!" Mom barks, interrupting me.

I'm so frustrated that I could grab that stupid doll and toss it out the window. I might, if I weren't so scared of it. Besides, Mom is glaring at me like I'm a rattlesnake and I know better than to keep talking.

"Sorry." I groan. I know it isn't Jonah's fault and I shouldn't be yelling at him, but part of me still feels angry. I'm just not sure who I'm angry at. Maybe it's him for liking that stupid doll. Maybe it's Mom and Dad for buying it for him. Couldn't they just have gotten him some Transformers or something like everyone else? Do they always have to stand out so much?

Mom sets a plate down in front of me and sighs. The smile she wore when I first came down is gone; now that she's standing beside me, I notice the faint bags under her eyes.

"I really am sorry. It was just a bad night." I try to sound sincere. The last person I want to make sad about this is Mom. She left all her painting behind, too. She lost her clients, her ocean . . . her everything. I don't want to make her feel worse. "And coming here where everything is so different is a little . . ."

"Overwhelming?" She pulls out a chair at the table and sits down. Then she nudges the plate in front of me closer.

There's no way I can eat.

"I know this is hard, Tessa," Mom says, draping a reassuring arm around my shoulders. "But your father and I . . . we're here for you. Anything you need, we're here."

I shake my head. "You don't know how hard it is. You can't. They aren't bothering you."

"Who?"

The ghosts.

"No one," I answer with a huff, and jump up, leaving behind the waffle and egg to get cold. I have to get to school. If I have any chance of figuring out who Inez is, and what Graceland is, and why that awful doll of Jonah's is tormenting me, I need to get to Nina. Fast.

16

Hi Rachel!

I'm sorry I haven't written you every day like I promised I would. There's just so much going on! I have good news and bad news. My house is officially haunted. That's obviously the bad news. The good news is that I'm actually making friends. Their names are Andrew, Nina, and Richie. Andrew is hilarious. You would really like him. And he plays soccer! Seriously, Nina tells me he's as crazy about it as you are. She's really nice and is super-smart about things like Chicago history and legends. And Richie is . . . well, he's a really good eater! JK, he's nice, too. I just hope this ghost stuff isn't too much weird for them, you know? I could really use some friends here—especially since I don't have you with me.

Love,

Tessa

The paper is smooth under my fingers. And completely blank, which I love. I slide my pastel downward to make a slate-gray streak that stops at the bottom edge of my sketchpad. It's perfect, so I do it again on the other side. Four more times and I'm staring at the outline of the three lockers sitting across from me.

They're cold and hard. Like everything else here. Well, everything except for North Pond. There, the sun was warm. The air smelled good and the water reminded me of Florida. It wasn't big, but it was something.

I pull myself upright, groaning. My back is to the wall and my butt is starting to go numb. I should be picking Nina's brain right now. Finding out what's going on in my house and what else she knows. Instead, I'm here, squished into a corner and hiding from the truth.

Maybe I'm afraid of what Nina will say. She could tell me something I haven't thought of yet. Something I don't want to know. An hour ago I couldn't wait to get here to tell her about the new drawing, and now I just want to forget about it.

"Florida? What are you doing?" Andrew's voice breaks through the quiet hall. He flips his cell phone from hand to hand and grins that crooked grin of his. "We were wondering where you were. Aren't you eating?"

Shaking my head, I try for a smile. "Nah. Not hungry."

In a few steps, Andrew is beside me. Today he's got on a soccer jersey. It's green and yellow and honestly . . . ugly. I stifle a laugh. Rachel and I used to make fun of the horrible tropical prints the old women back in Fort Myers wore, but this jersey is so much worse. It looks like a banana threw up green beans.

"What are you laughing at?" He looks down at me suspiciously for a minute, then slides down the wall and settles onto the floor beside me.

I shrug and try to keep myself from staring at his phone. Why can't my parents just let me have one, too? Or even a laptop! Then I could talk to Rachel. I could research this stuff on my own.

I could figure out what Graceland is.

"Hey!" Andrew says, snapping his fingers in front of my face. "Anyone home?"

"I'm fine. Just having a weird day." Meeting his

eyes, I add, "And if you insist on calling me Florida, or Surfer Girl, or any other nickname like that, I'm going to start calling you . . . well, I don't know what yet, but you won't like it!"

"Seriously? What's so wrong with me calling you Florida?" he asks, watching me intently. "You kind of *are* Florida. I mean, you're so tan and you have that long rumpled-up hair."

By *rumpled-up,* I assume he means that my hair is wavy. Which is true. Occasionally back home I'd twist it into a bun so it didn't get all knotted up by the sun and wind and sand. But not always. Sometimes it felt good to leave it loose, free to whip around my face and shield my eyes from the glare of the water.

Something stirs inside me, dark and sad. "Whatever. Just . . . just don't call me that."

Andrew's face twists into a look of apology. "Hey, I'm sorry. I won't call you that anymore if it actually upsets you. I thought you were kidding." He goes quiet and looks thoughtful for a moment. "That nickname isn't why you skipped lunch, is it?"

I put all my energy into holding back the tears. I refuse to cry. "It's not that. I'm just having a bad day."

"Is this a 'girl problem' like hair and stuff, or is it an actual problem?"

His eyes skip over my sketchpad and I instinctively

flip it closed. I shoot him a steely look. "For the record, saying 'girl problem' makes you sound like a jerk."

Andrew looks deflated for a moment. His mouth is hanging open like a fish gasping for breath on the shore.

"Oh, come on! I make one little joke you don't like and now I can't look at your art?" His voice cracks a little, and even though he's smiling again, I can tell he's a little hurt. I feel bad. I'm not trying to shut him out and it definitely wasn't the joke that made me close my sketchpad.

Jeez. I'm hurting everyone today.

"It's not finished. I never show my work until it's finished. Otherwise it just looks like a mess to people." I tell myself this is only a half-lie. Not a whole one.

"O-kay. That still doesn't explain why you're being such a creeper out here instead of with us at lunch. Today is Thursday . . . your fourth day here and you still don't seem any more comfortable than on day one. Everything okay?"

"Yeah . . . no. I don't know."

Andrew tips his head to the side. "Spill it."

His eyes flick toward the large clock at the end of the hall before coming back to rest on mine. "We've got science in ten minutes and Ms. Geist isn't going to start class late for your 'girl problems.'" Andrew says this with a goofy smirk and I can tell how hard he's trying to lighten my mood.

I punch him in the arm, laughing. Andrew really does have a funny sense of humor. If it weren't for all the stuff going on at home, this would actually be a decent day here. A good one. And in Chicago. Weird.

I stuff my sketchpad into my backpack, taking a deep breath. I have two choices: tell Andrew what happened in my room last night and risk him thinking I really am batty, or keep it to myself and suffer silently. I really, really hate to suffer.

"Okay, but I think we're going to need Nina."

17

SCHOOL ENDED OVER AN HOUR AGO, AND I'M still sitting on the front steps watching cars race by in a blur. People drove fast in Florida, but they didn't drive this fast. And they didn't honk this much, either.

"I told you I'm walking as fast as I can!" Nina appears in the doorway of the school, and Andrew is only a step behind her. She doesn't look as shy this time. In fact, she looks annoyed.

There's something about Nina that reminds me a little of Rachel. It definitely isn't her hair or her skin. Maybe it's the way she walks or the way she talks. It's something nice, though, and despite the fact that she's still shooting lasers at Andrew with her eyes, I smile. "Hey."

"Hey yourself. Mr. Bossypants here dragged me out of Film Club. It only happens once a week—on Wednesdays—and Andrew here walked in right in the middle of it!" Nina punctuates the last few words with a jab to his ribs and he winces.

"I'm sorry. I just needed to talk to you and he knew how to find you," I say, suddenly feeling more guilty than worried. Maybe I shouldn't have bothered her with this.

"No, it's fine. We were discussing *The Watcher in the Woods* and I've seen that a million times anyway." She mumbles this last part. I can already feel her closing up on me again.

I need to get her talking quick or I'll lose her. "Have you ever heard of somewhere called Graceland?"

Nina's eyes pop wide and for a moment, her jaw is slack. "Graceland? Why?"

I shoot a nervous glance at Andrew and he circles a hand in the air like I should keep going. "C'mon. Spit it out, Tessa. I didn't nearly get torn to shreds pulling her out of Film Club for nothing."

Inhaling, I continue. "Remember how I told you there's something going on in my house?"

Nina nods, and the three of us take a seat on the steps. She shoves her backpack behind us and leans in closer to me. "I'm confused. How could the things going on in your house have anything to do with Graceland?"

I toss my hands in the air. "I don't know what in the heck Graceland is, so how can I answer that?"

"Isn't that where Elvis lived?" Andrew pipes up.

"Shhhhhh!" Nina hisses, and looks around. I can't be certain, but I think it's to make sure no one is listening.

Snatching up her backpack and unzipping it, Nina begins digging around for something. When her hands reappear, there's a book in them: *The Ghosts of Chicago*.

"Oh my god. Is Graceland a building? Did my parents buy a haunted house called Graceland?" I begin to panic, wondering if this might be why my dad kept saying our house was a "steal." If someone died there, they'd probably lower the price . . . right?

Nina waves me off. "No. Graceland is a cemetery just north of Wrigley Field. It's one of the two cemeteries that took the bodies they dug up and relocated from Lincoln Park."

A cemetery. I think about this and a sudden chill washes over me. Nina is in some kind of crazy-excited mode where she's talking a million miles a minute, but I really can't focus. I just keep hearing that one word over and over again: *cemetery.* Whatever ghost is trapped in my house is sending me a message, and it has something to do with Graceland Cemetery.

But why is it trying to reach me?

Watching Nina chatter away, I suddenly realize something about her. She seems so quiet—so timid when she isn't talking about ghosts. But the minute anything paranormal comes up . . . boom! Nina starts talking. Maybe that's what reminds me of Rachel. Her sudden bursts of excitement. Nina's excitement isn't about soccer, like Rachel's was, but about ghosts and graveyards and bodies lost underneath the ground. It might be odd, but it's familiar and I can't help but like it.

"So, you understand?" Nina finishes, and I realize I didn't hear a word she just said.

"She wasn't listening." Andrew groans.

"How do you know that?" I ask.

He snorts and exchanges a look with Nina. "When she's tuning you out, she gets that spacey look in her eyes. I saw her do it at the park while she was drawing."

"You were spying on me?" I playfully drop both hands to my hips and wait for his answer. I thought Andrew went home with his dad that day. He even told me he did. Now I find out he was probably crouched down in a bush or something, watching me?

"Not spying! I just watched for a minute. From a distance." Andrew looks uncomfortable as he fidgets with the edges of his jersey. "You looked so happy and I wanted to come see what you were drawing, but—"

"Yeah, yeah. You had to go. But not before you spied on me!" I fight the urge to smile. I really don't like having my privacy invaded, but I'm discovering that it's hard to *actually* be angry with Andrew. Especially when the sun is lighting up his ocean eyes again.

"It wasn't spying!" Andrew yells out.

Just then, the door to the school opens and Cassidy walks out. She's wearing skinny jeans and a black jacket, making her blue streak stand out even more.

"Cass!" Andrew shouts, catching her attention. "You gotta go home?"

She glances at me hesitantly. "Not until four thirty. Why?"

"Sweet. We're gonna hang out here for a little while. Maybe you could stay?"

For the first time since I've met her, something other than a frown settles on Cassidy's face. It's not quite a smile, but she doesn't look like she just swallowed a toad, either.

Finally shrugging her backpack off her shoulders, she sets it on the ground. "Um. Yeah. I think I can do that."

"Awesome! Pull up a step." Andrew sweeps his arms out over the stairs.

I stare at the ground, suddenly understanding what it means to feel like a third wheel. Andrew is so happy that Cassidy is staying, but all I can think about is how I'm going to survive the next hour with her around. Maybe she *is* actually a nice person. Maybe she *can* be super-fun to be around. Maybe there *are* tons of reasons why Andrew, Nina, and Richie hang out with her. But if any of that is true, Cassidy has a lot of work to do for me to believe it.

Sitting down, Cassidy pulls her knees up to her chest. "So. What are we going to do? There isn't time to bowl or anything like that, but we could go to Yoberri."

"Actually, we're going to help Tessa *not* be the star of the next *Paranormal Activity* movie." Andrew chuckles. "Got any suggestions?"

Cassidy's shoulders stiffen. "Help Tessa," she repeats.

"Her house is haunted," Nina says matter-of-factly. She's digging through a book, marking different pages with bright orange Post-it notes. "Clue number one is Graceland Cemetery."

"Of course," Cass quips. "I forgot about her haunted house."

She looks from Andrew to Nina, then finally to me. Her blue eyes are icy, *angry* as she gathers her backpack up off the steps. "You know, I think I do have to go home. Sorry. Orthodontist appointment."

Andrew scoffs. "Orthodontist? What are you talking about? You don't even have braces!"

"Well, I might someday and I want to be prepared," she responds, staring at Andrew pointedly. I notice that she doesn't sound guilty this time. She sounds mad.

Nina flips her book closed. I half expect her to shrink back, fade into the bushes rather than facing Cassidy's anger, but she doesn't. Instead she slowly shakes her head.

"What is that?" Cassidy demands. "Why are you shaking your head at me like that?"

"Because you're kind of throwing a fit," Nina retorts.

Cassidy's mouth goes slack.

Nina clears her throat, her expression softening. "I'm sorry. I shouldn't have said that. It's just that you're acting so . . . so . . ."

"So *what*?" Cass asks.

"So un-Cassidy! Where is that crazy hyena laugh of yours? Where are all the fun new lipstick samples? Where are all your cool stories about the cities you've visited and the wristbands you bought?" Nina pauses, her pale face growing more worried by the second. "Where is *Cassidy*?"

Hyena laugh? Lipstick samples? Cool stories? Holy cow. I have a great imagination, but those things don't match up with the Cassidy I know at all.

"Tell us what's going on," Nina begs. *"Please."*

Cassidy takes a deep breath, looking pained. For a minute I think she might finally volunteer something. But then her eyes jump back to me again.

"No. I'm going home."

18

WE'RE ALL SILENT. NINA IS WATCHING CASSIDY disappear around the bend in the road. Andrew's mouth is gaping open.

Time to talk about the elephant in the room, or so my dad would say. "So. She really hates me. Not just a little hate, either . . . a full-on, wish-you'd-fall-off-the-edge-of-a-cliff hate."

Andrew shoots me an apologetic look. "I'm sorry, Tessa. Cass isn't being fair."

"Don't apologize." I feel bad for Andrew. It isn't his fault that Cassidy would obviously rather fall into a tank of electric eels than hang out with me, but based on the way she steamed past him like she just robbed a bank, I think she blames him anyway.

"I don't get it," Nina says. "I keep thinking things are going to go back to normal any day now. But they seem worse."

"Worse since I showed up?"

The look on their faces is all the answer I need. I sigh. As if it isn't bad enough to have a ghost waiting for me at home, now I have this to worry about. *Cassidy.* As long as I'm around, Andrew, Nina, and Richie are losing their friend. It isn't right, but I don't know how to fix it.

Nina looks down at her phone and groans. "Guys, I know no one wants to hear this right now, but we're running out of time."

"Right. Back to Graceland," Andrew says quickly. He tries to sound cheerful, but it's impossible to miss the sadness in his tone. This thing with Cassidy is really bothering him.

"Back to Graceland," I say halfheartedly.

Nina jumps up from her spot on the steps. "Let's walk somewhere. I don't want to talk about this stuff here. Too many people around."

Agreed. The kids here probably already think I'm weird because of what I said about my house being haunted. I don't need to make it worse. And Nina . . . I'm beginning to understand why she's so quiet most of the time. Ghosts aren't a hobby for many twelve-year-olds.

"Where do you guys want to go?" Andrew asks.

I think about it for a minute. We can't go to my house, not unless I want my friends to be scared away before we can even start researching. And I have no clue where the library is. "How about North Pond?"

"Perfect," he says, pulling a jacket on and zipping up. "There's always a few artists there with their canvases, but there's never anyone from our school."

Something tugs at my heart and I almost stop walking. I'd love nothing more than to curl up at North Pond with my pastels and draw. Maybe finish my water lilies. Or start something new, like the fountain I passed on my way to the pond the first time I was there. But none of that can happen until I get rid of this ghost!

I haven't realized how close North Pond actually is to our school until I see the fiery-colored trees and small walking trails. I steer us toward the dock again, hoping it's empty and we can just chill there.

"The dock?" Nina asks as we take our first few steps onto it. "It's a little dirty, don't you think?" She skirts around a pile of what I assume is goose poop and grimaces.

"She likes the water," Andrew chimes in.

I stop walking and stare at him. "Why do you keep answering questions about me?"

A faint blush creeps into Andrew's cheeks and he looks away. "I don't know. You're different."

"Great. Different. Something every new girl wants to hear," I grumble.

"No! I don't mean it that way. I mean you're interesting. I've never known anyone from Florida and I definitely don't know any real artists."

Real artists? His words echo in my ears, filling me with excitement. Andrew thinks I'm a real artist. No one my own age has ever said that before. Then again, I guess I haven't really given them the chance. Back in Florida I didn't share my artwork with anyone other than Mom and Dad.

Nina clears her throat, pulling me from my thoughts. She's settled down at the end of the dock and is sitting cross-legged with the book in her hands. I follow her, sweeping several feathers into the water with the toe of my shoe before plunking down.

"So. You need to tell me everything. I mean *everything*," Nina says.

"I asked about Graceland because last night, something woke me up. It was crying. Then there were footsteps and my doorknob was rattling."

My heart is hammering against my ribs as I remember it. The darkness and the sounds. The feeling that something was in that hallway, trying to get to me. It was horrible.

Nina and Andrew look unfazed. They sit silently, waiting for me to continue.

"Then my little brother's doll looked like it was crying. It said 'Graceland' over and over again."

Andrew flinches. "The doll was crying? And talking? You mean you saw it or you heard it? Were your eyes open?"

The questions are coming so fast I hold my hand up to stop him. "Yes to all of those. I heard it *and* saw it. And before you ask, yes, I was awake."

"Was that the end of it?" Nina asks quietly. She's flipping through the book now and doesn't stop until she lands on the chapter titled "Graceland Cemetery."

I shake my head. "The next morning, there was an addition to the pastel drawing that keeps showing up in my sketchpad. It's the outline of a girl. I'm positive. Underneath, it says 'Inez.'"

I take a deep breath and watch for their reactions. Andrew looks concerned but blank. Like he doesn't have a clue who or what Inez is. Nina, however, looks petrified. Her face is even more ashen than it usually is and her eyes are dark. Scared.

"Inez?" she whispers, clutching the book tighter

until her knuckles turn white. "Are you sure? Did you bring it?"

"Yes. I'm positive it says 'Inez.' But I didn't bring it. I didn't want it in my backpack all day. I couldn't stand the thought of it being that close to me."

Nina looks at Andrew, then back at me. Her chestnut hair flutters away from her face with the breeze, then settles back across her shoulders. "Inez Clarke was six years old and lived here in Chicago. She's one of the most famous Chicago ghost legends ever."

"She can't be that famous," Andrew says quizzically. "I haven't heard of her."

"If it isn't round, black and white, and stitched together, you haven't heard of it." Nina laughs.

Andrew mimics her laughter and bends down to look at the Graceland heading. "So is she buried there? Is that the connection?"

The small hairs on the back of my neck are standing at attention again and I smooth them down. I want to know what's going on in my house, but I was hoping I'd feel less afraid once I did. That definitely isn't happening.

"Yes and no," Nina answers. "The legend is that Inez was accidentally locked out of her house by her parents during a storm and killed by lightning." She flips to a different page and holds the book in front of my face.

What I see takes my breath away. It isn't a traditional grave, at least not like one I've ever seen before. Instead it's a glass box, with a beautiful statue of a little girl perched inside it. The same box that showed up in my sketchpad. The same little girl drawn inside. And the same name etched into the cement. INEZ.

19

I STARE AT THE BOX, CONFUSED. INEZ CLARKE. Is she the little girl I heard crying last night in our hallways? And if so, why is she haunting my house?

"Is that the picture in your sketchpad?" Nina asks.

"Yeah," I say, tracing the lines of the glass box with my index finger. "That's it for sure."

Confusion grips me. If Inez is the ghost in my house, why was Reno talking and crying? It makes no sense.

"Why me? Why my house?"

I'm shaking now and I can't help it. It's one thing to know there's a ghost in my house, but it's another thing altogether to discover it's a dead six-year-old girl.

Andrew puts a hand on my shoulder. The teasing

smirk is gone and now he looks reassuring. "Hey, before you get too freaked out, remember that none of this is necessarily true."

I toss my hands into the air, exasperated. "She's a graveyard expert, Andrew! Of course it's true!"

Nina shakes her head. "I'm not an expert. It just happens to be something that interests me. That's all. And there's a catch to this story, anyway. One I can't explain."

"What?" Andrew and I ask at the same time.

Nina looks back down at the lifelike cement image of the girl staring up from the glossy page of her book. "There was no Inez Clarke."

"What?" I close my eyes for a moment so I can recall the statue. The dates inscribed under it. Glancing down at the page Nina is pointing to, I see them in black and white.

INEZ CLARKE
SEPTEMBER 20, 1873
AUGUST 1, 1880

If Inez Clarke didn't exist, what were those dates? Why would there even be a statue?

Nina points to a highlighted paragraph in the book. "This says that according to the cemetery records at Graceland, Inez Clarke isn't even buried there. But that's not all. . . . There was no Inez Clarke in the Chicago census, either."

"That makes no sense. It says her name right there on the statue!" Andrew objects, jabbing a finger at the book.

"I know. But the cemetery records show a little boy buried there, named Amos Briggs." Nina sighs.

I try to wrap my tired brain around this. Ghosts are supposed to be tortured souls, right? So how can Inez be one if she never existed to begin with?

Andrew looks like he's caught somewhere between *holy crap* and *I'm outta here.* "Whoa, whoa, whoa. Slow down. Let's just look at the facts. Inez Clarke is the name on the gravestone."

Nina twists the thin black leather bracelet she wears around her wrist over and over again. "Correct."

"But the City of Chicago says no one lived here at that time with that name?" he continues, looking more disturbed by the moment.

Nina purses her lips into a tight line and rolls her shoulders. "Also correct."

"Well, one of those is obviously wrong. What else do you know?" I ask Nina, picking up the book with trembling hands.

"Nothing. I'm sorry."

"But . . . but you're the graveyard expert!" I sputter out. "You have to know! I need you to know!" The tug-of-war between my imagination and my common sense begins. And right now, my imagination is winning.

Nina shifts uncomfortably on the dock. "Listen, my parents aren't exactly big fans of my graveyard hobby. It creeps Mom out, and—well, my dad loves history, but not enough to drive me to cemeteries every weekend."

"So what are you saying?" I ask.

"I'm saying I don't own *every* book and visit *every* graveyard and research *every* ghost. I can't! Not unless I want my parents to think I'm even weirder than they already do."

Her voice tapers off a little at the end and my heart sinks. Nina seems so smart. She's nice, too. It makes me sad to think that her parents don't notice that. It also scares me, because if Nina doesn't know more about Inez . . . no one does. And that means I'm in a *lot* of trouble.

Nina looks between Andrew and me somberly. "Forget about my parents. They're . . . it's all good. It isn't possible to know *everything* about all the Chicago ghost legends, anyway. There's Resurrection Mary, the *Eternal Silence* statue, the Red Lion Pub. . . . There's too many! Besides what I've already told you, Inez is a mystery to me."

"It sounds like she's a mystery to everyone," I say numbly. Disappointment floods me from the inside out. Short of a miracle, I have no idea how I'm going to get rid of this ghost.

"Field trip!" Andrew says, popping up from his spot and startling me. He's bouncing on the balls of his feet like he's about to enter a boxing ring. "Graceland, here we come!"

"What? No! No way," I say immediately.

Andrew grips my shoulders and gives them a gentle shake. "Yes way. How else are you going to end this, Florida?" The nickname slips out and he suddenly looks worried.

"It's okay. I have bigger things to worry about than that stupid nickname," I say. "I want to end this, but if you're suggesting we prowl around Graceland Cemetery—"

"He's right. We need to go there," Nina says, stuffing the book back in her backpack. "The cemetery's front office will know more about this than we can find in books. If we can get them to talk to us, we might have a chance at figuring out what she wants."

What she wants. The words bounce around in my head like a possessed Ping-Pong ball. Does Inez want something from me?

I stay frozen in place, the reality of my situation sinking in. Out of the millions of people in Chicago, for some reason this ghost has chosen me.

I look up at the rapidly dropping sun.

"You guys would really do this for me? Go into that cemetery?" My voice cracks slightly as I ask the question. I can't help it. I'm a little overwhelmed. Back home, Rachel was the only one who would have done something like this for me. And even then, she had her limits. But Andrew and Nina seem so determined to help me that I almost feel guilty.

Nina's eyes soften. "Of course. You're having a bad time and you need help right now. You need *friends.*"

I grin. I do need friends. Everyone does. My thoughts shift back to Cassidy. I can't help but think about the way her shoulders hunch over and her mouth turns downward when she thinks no one is looking. Is that what she needs, too? Friends? I shake off the thought, wishing I'd never met her to begin with. Cassidy obviously doesn't want anything to do with me, but *still.* I can't stop wondering why.

"Okay. So we go to Graceland. But not now. I'm

not going there unless it's bright and sunny outside." I sneak a glance at the screen of Nina's cell phone. It's 5:15 right now. The sun sets early here, so early that in the next hour the streetlights will begin flickering on. I won't go to Graceland in the dark. I can't.

Nina pauses, looking thoughtful. "Agreed. We might want pictures or at least detailed notes, so there's no point in going there when it's getting too dark anyway. Plus, I think the gates close at some point every day."

Thank goodness for that, I think. Otherwise Andrew and his wild ideas would get us all in trouble.

Nina thumps her sneakered foot against the dock as if she's thinking. "Saturday, then. Today is Wednesday, so hopefully whatever's happening in your house doesn't get much worse by then. Meet here at eight a.m. and bring your bikes. We'll go to the front office. Hopefully they'll answer some questions about Inez."

"And Amos Briggs," Andrew adds. "I'm supposed to be at soccer Saturday, but if you guys think I can help, I'll skip."

Nina raises an eyebrow. "You? Skip soccer? Who are you and what have you done with the Andrew who would marry a soccer ball if it were legal?"

"Shut up," Andrew mumbles. Still, he can't keep the smile from creeping onto his face. A smile that reminds me of how lucky I am.

I shoot a silent thank-you to the universe. Then I start trying to prepare myself for the trip we've all agreed to make.

20

THERE'S NOTHING IN MY ROOM. THERE'S NOTHING in my room. There's nothing in my room. I put this phrase on repeat in my mind, hoping it will slow down my racing heart, but something tells me it isn't going to help.

It's funny, I can almost make myself forget about the ghost in our house when we're all at dinner—Dad mimicking Grandma and her opinions about "the big city" and Mom laughing so hard she has to stop eating so she doesn't choke. I can even overlook the fact that Jonah is still allowed to bring Reno to the table—even though that doll almost gave me a heart attack!

But at night . . . late at night when the whole house is asleep, that's when things get ugly. I close my eyes and hear stuff. Creaks. Thumps. Even the darkness has a sound of its own, and I hate it.

I jump out of my bed and yank all the covers off. Wrapping them around me mummy-like, I head into the hallway. My breath catches in my throat as I stand there for a moment, squinting into the pitch black. This sucks. I can't sleep in my room, but taking my chances with our terrifying stairwell doesn't sound much better. I imagine a bony hand reaching out of the dark and snagging my ankle, or Reno's gaping wooden mouth hissing my name, or the crackling. I hate the crackling.

Stay calm, Tess. Just stay calm.

Easing down the first couple of steps, I notice that the painting hanging in the stairwell is crooked. Not just a little crooked, either. It's *about to fall off the wall* crooked. I inch closer, cursing myself for not being able to ignore it. In this house, I'm probably the only one who would notice, anyway. Mom still spends a lot of time hunting for her missing water-colors, Dad is busy practicing his new music, and Jonah . . . yeah, Jonah has Reno. The doll that never takes a vacation.

Even in the dark, I can tell the picture has changed again. The paint colors are so deep that they're almost black now, and the flowers are gnarled and brown.

Dead. My hands shake as I reach out to straighten the edges.

A dark smudge appears in the corner of the picture where I just touched it—a smudge that wasn't there before. I pull my finger back and squint through the darkness, holding my breath. Paint. My finger is covered in wet paint.

Scrambling away from the painting, I grab the railing, then stagger down the rest of the steps. Inez did that to the painting. She had to! Mom would never touch up another artist's work like that, and there's no other explanation for it. Just like there's no other explanation for the drawing in my sketchpad.

When I finally reach the living room, I'm such a shaky mess that I almost cry. How did things end up like this? Everyone else is sound asleep, probably having good dreams, and here I am . . . alone and shaking in a house I'm terrified of. I wipe the reddish-black paint off my finger onto my pajama pants, not even caring that it will probably never come out. Then I start turning on all the lamps. I need light, and lots of it.

Once every lamp we own is turned on, I plop down on the couch under Mom's paintings and pull my knees up to my chin. The sudden brightness hurts my eyes but feels good at the same time. Safe.

Yup. Until I find out for sure what Inez Clarke

wants from me, this is where I'll be sleeping. With the lights on, of course.

I wake up with a start. Fear trickles into me like slivers of ice as I glance toward the window. It's still dark outside. Still nighttime. I'm in the same spot where I fell asleep—the couch in the living room—and I don't hear any crying or moaning or doorknob rattling. The house is quiet.

So why did I wake up?

Sitting up, I scan the room. There're a few stray boxes still waiting to be unpacked, a mountain of Jonah's Lego toys in the middle of the rug, and a stack of Dad's sheet music sitting on the table. So far so good. Nothing unusual.

Then my eyes skip across the floor. I freeze. There's a scattering of something there, at the base of the brick wall. Dirt? Graham cracker crumbs from Jonah? I shake my head, remembering how hard I tried to convince Mom and Dad to tear that dumb wall out before we moved in. I told them how weird it is to have a brick wall *inside* our house, and that it was just one more thing about Chicago that felt cold and creepy. They said it was vintage architecture and we were lucky to get it. Right. Lucky.

I drag myself off the couch and crawl over, curious.

As soon as I get close I realize it isn't even dirt. It's dark red dust. There are some bigger chunks of brick in it, like the wall is crumbling. Huh. My parents were here for an entire day before they bought the house while some guy inspected it for problems. He told them about the pipes and the old water heater. He even told them about the tiny crack in the kitchen window. But he missed this? I mean, he should have noticed it, right?

Unless it wasn't there. . . .

My stomach does a flip-flop. Maybe this is another clue.

I swallow hard, wishing my friends were here. They'd know what to do and they wouldn't be as scared as I am. Especially Nina. She definitely wouldn't pretend she didn't see the dust and just go back to sleep like I was thinking about doing. *No.* She'd investigate. I should investigate.

Placing my palms against the wall, I follow the line of bricks straight up from the dust pile. One at a time, I press on them. Press, wiggle. Press, wiggle. Press, wiggle. The fifth brick up from the floor crackles when I touch it. I knock on it gently, gasping as more dust rains down onto the floor. I found it. I found the loose brick! A lightbulb goes on in my brain; I know exactly what I need to do.

With shaking hands, I grip the rough edges of the

brick and start jiggling it back and forth. It grows looser and looser in its spot until it feels like I could slide it out entirely.

Here goes nothing.

I slide the brick out, mesmerized by the yawning black hole left in the wall. I want to know if I'm right and there's something hidden in there, but not bad enough to stick my hand in. I've seen way too many scary movies to do something dumb like that.

I make a mental note to tell Mom and Dad about this when it's all over. I don't just want a phone anymore. I need one. If I had one right now, I'd be able to use the flashlight on it to see inside the gap. Now I'm stuck with either searching the house for a flashlight (no thank you), trying to sneak into Mom and Dad's room to get one of their phones (double no thank you), or using a lamp.

I settle for the lamp. Placing it on the floor, I angle the shade so that all the light is aimed at the hole in the wall. Then I creep back to the hole and peer in. There are some yellowed papers tucked deep inside. They're tied up with twine.

Hesitantly, I reach in and grab them. The second my fingers touch the brittle paper I gasp. The memory of what woke me up is back, and it isn't just scary. It's *terrifying.*

21

I REPLAY THE SOUND IN MY HEAD OVER AND over again as I sit there on the floor, clutching the rolled-up papers. It was a slow scrape, followed by a clink. The sound of a brick being shoved back into the wall. I'm sure of it.

Standing up on shaky legs, I grab the brick and tuck it back into its original spot. Then I peel the corner of our rug up and use my sock to sweep the dust underneath it. I don't want Mom and Dad to know about that loose brick. Not yet. Maybe not ever, depending on what's written on the papers I found behind it. Papers hidden in an ancient wall can't be good. It's like a teacher asking to speak with *both* parents at midterms, or the lunch lady bragging about sauerkraut being on the menu. All kinds of bad.

Crouching down next to the lamp, I straighten the shade and carefully begin to untie the twine. The paper is so old that it stays rolled up even when the twine is removed. Slowly, I flatten it out on the floor, then use four of Jonah's bigger Legos to pin down the corners.

It's another pastel drawing, but this time it isn't of a grave. It looks like a room. I blink at it, trailing my index finger over the simple lines that make up the dresser and the bed. I move the Legos and switch to the next paper. The drawing on that one is of a rectangle. A rectangle on tiny legs. At first I think it might be an old-fashioned bathtub with feet like ours, but then I notice the line at the top. The rectangle looks like it should open. Plus, there are a few crooked flowers outlined on each corner. I've never seen a bathtub—even an old one—with flowers on it.

A dozen different possibilities flash through my brain: toy box, clothes hamper, suitcase. They end with one—a possibility that sends a chill from the base of my spine up to the top of my head: a music box. Could that be it? It's hard to tell because like in the first drawing, the lines aren't perfect. They're crude. Unfinished.

They're exactly what they would look like if a six-year-old drew them.

In an instant, the goose bumps are back. Did Inez draw these? And if she did, what is she trying to tell me with them?

Flipping the pages over one at a time, I examine the letters scrawled onto the back—*I. B.* Interesting. Most artists place their mark, or initials, or signature somewhere on their work. These look like initials, and if they are, my mystery just got a lot more confusing, because the last name of the little girl I *thought* was haunting me doesn't start with *B*.

I roll the drawings back up and retie the twine. My eyes are heavy and my head hurts. Crawling back onto the couch, I take one more look at the wall. Thankfully, the brick hasn't moved.

"I'll figure it out," I whisper, a yawn taking over. "I promise. I just need a little sleep." *And a lot of time,* I think. Based on the clues this ghost is leaving, even the *Scooby-Doo* gang would be confused.

22

IT'S FINALLY SATURDAY. GRAVEYARD DAY. I kept hoping something would change—that Inez would stop haunting me and we wouldn't even need to come here, but it hasn't happened. Thursday and Friday were just as bad as every other day since we moved into the house on Shady Street. Maybe even worse.

Thursday I spent the night searching the house with Mom. We were trying to find her lost watercolors. No luck. The only thing we found was Reno . . . in my room . . . *again*. Jonah swore he didn't put him there and I know he's telling the truth, which only leaves one possibility. Inez. Then last night a gust of wind woke me up. It was so strong that it knocked one of Mom's paintings off the wall. Fortunately, it landed on the couch and not my head, but yikes.

Inez is definitely still around. She's also definitely still unhappy.

I know I agreed to come here, but now that we're standing in front of the gates to Graceland Cemetery, I'm having second thoughts.

"So. I guess it's go time," Andrew says, his face tilted upward toward the sky. Black clouds drift lazily across the palette of grays. Low rumbles echo in the distance.

I laugh to myself. Of course it's stormy and scary-looking on the day we visit the graveyard. Why wouldn't it be?

The gates are thick black wrought iron and they're wide open. Enormous trees stretch as far as I can see. "Let's just get this over with." I groan, pulling my jacket tighter up around my neck. The wind is biting into me today and I don't want to be outside—here—any longer than we have to be.

"I think the offices for the cemetery are just to the right," Nina whispers as we cross through the gates and find ourselves on a narrow paved path.

"Why are you whispering?" Andrew asks. "It's not like you're going to bother any of them." With this, he sweeps his hand over the gravestones sprawled out in front of us.

For a moment I can't breathe. There. Are. So. Many. Huge ones that spiral up to the sky and small ones that are chipped and unmarked. Ones with faces, and ones with entire bodies carved into the stone. Maybe they're supposed to immortalize someone or make us feel better about death, but all they make me want to do is pee my pants.

A smile fills out Nina's pale face. She cinches her dark blue jacket tighter around her neck and nods toward the graves. "Welcome to Graceland, guys."

The excitement in her voice is hard to miss. Even with all the hair whipping around in her face, I can see it too. Her hot-cocoa-colored eyes are bright, twinkling like she just stepped through the gates of Disney World. Only this isn't Disney World. It's a freaking cemetery and I've never been so nervous in my whole life.

A small brick building sits in the corner, exactly where Nina said it was. It looks newer than all the headstones surrounding it—out of place almost. The door is, of course, locked, and there's a small buzzer. I push it with shaking hands and wait for the door to unlatch so we can go in. There we find a small, lobby-like room with a couch and two leather armchairs. There are black-and-white pictures framed on the walls, and brochures about choosing Graceland as a final resting place.

"Can I help you?" A woman's voice breaks into the quiet and all three of us snap to attention. Nina composes herself first.

"Yes. We're here looking for the grave of Inez Clarke." Her voice trembles just slightly, giving away that even our local graveyard expert is a little afraid. "Can you tell us which direction it is?"

The woman nods and tucks a pen behind her ear. The tip of it peeks out of her salt-and-pepper hair just enough to look like some kind of weird barrette. She slides open a drawer behind her desk and rifles through it for a moment. Then she ambles over to the counter and sets a sheet of paper down in front of us. It looks like a map, only instead of cities and states, there are numbers.

"The cemetery is divided up into a series of different paths with street names." She traces one with her finger, then highlights it in bright pink. I'm surprised they have pink highlighters in graveyard offices. You'd think they'd stick with something uglier.

"This path is called Main Street. Take that until you hit Graceland Avenue and veer left. That will take you directly to Inez's grave site."

Graceland Avenue in Graceland Cemetery. Interesting.

"So the person actually buried here is someone

by the name of Amos Briggs—is that right? A little boy?" Nina asks, tapping on the number forty-two, which indicates where the statue of Inez Clarke is. She's getting braver.

The woman's eyebrows knit together tightly. She turns and looks through the window, scouring the scene outside for something. "Are you here with a tour group? Because they are required to register in advance with us!" Her tone is sharp now and I'm worried. Maybe we shouldn't be asking anything at all.

Andrew steps up to the counter and smiles. He looks so innocent when he does that. "No, ma'am. We're not here with a ghost tour. We're here because we're doing a research project. Inez Clarke is very important to us. Can you help?"

She studies his face for a moment. The wrinkles in her forehead slowly smooth out and disappear. "If you're asking me to tell you the truth, I will. I don't know for sure if Inez Clarke is buried there. I know *someone* is buried there and the name Amos Briggs is on the plot record. But the statue says 'Inez.'"

A clap of thunder shakes the building and Nina shrieks. The woman gasps and the lights flicker.

I close my eyes for a brief moment and try to steady my breathing. The first time the lights flickered on me anywhere, it was in my bathroom at home, and that ended up being one of the most terrifying experience of my life. Then they flickered again—in my room. Why does this keep happening around me?

"I can also tell you that there have been reports of the statue disappearing." The woman's voice drops until she's nearly whispering. "Grounds keepers for generations have reported that it vanishes during lightning storms."

"V-Vanishes?" I stutter. "How is that possible?"

The woman shrugs, a wicked smile stretching across her wrinkled face. "I don't know, dear. I'm only telling you what I've heard through the grapevine. Apparently, shortly after Inez's statue showed up in the cemetery, the storms started."

Storms. There *have* been a lot of storms since I moved to Chicago.

"Terrible storms with the kind of thunder and lightning that rattle your bones," she continues. Her voice is raspy. *Scary.*

"Any other, um, strange things happen around the statue?" I swallow hard, half afraid to hear her answer.

She nods and the pen behind her ear bobs. "You name it and it's happened. But the crying . . . the crying is the worst."

My ears perk up. "Crying?"

"Oh, yes. Sometimes, just before we close the

gates, we hear someone crying. It sounds like a girl. A little girl." She pulls the pen from behind her ear and slowly draws a bright red circle around the location of Inez's grave. "Maybe even Inez."

Nina looks at me nervously. The lights flicker once, twice, three more times before resuming full strength. *Please don't let them go out completely,* I think. I can't handle being stuck in a cemetery office in the pitch black. Especially with this woman.

"Vanishing statue. Storms. Crying. Got it," Nina says, digging a pen from her bag and jotting down a note on the side of the graveyard map. "All of that definitely backs up the story that Inez died of a lightning strike. I mean, the haunted part of it makes sense."

"Was Amos Briggs listed in the Chicago census at the time? I mean, was he a real person?" Andrew asks.

I turn to look at him, impressed. I hadn't thought of it, but he's brought up a good question.

"I'm not sure, dear. I'm sorry. I don't usually answer questions about the older grave sites like Inez's. I'm more of a liaison to the families that are considering burying their loved ones here now."

"Thank you for your time. And for the map," Nina says, taking my hand and dragging me toward the door.

We step outside just in time for a gust of wind to hit us, sending the map sailing into the air. Andrew chases after it, raising his fist in victory as he plants a wet heel on it to pin it down.

Nina peels it off the pavement. "Inez Clarke's grave is really not that far from where we are now."

"No way," I say, shaking my head violently. "It's going to start pouring any minute and if we get stuck there during a storm, they might need to start digging a hole for me!"

Andrew rubs the back of his neck and scans the sky. "If you really don't want to, it's okay, but I think we have time."

Orange leaves rain down, then plaster themselves to the wet pavement. The partially bare tree limbs rattle against one another in the wind, making me think of bones . . . all the bones tucked down in the soggy earth around us. I hold my breath as another stiff breeze howls across the stretch of headstones, bringing with it the smell of burning wood. A fireplace.

What I wouldn't give to be back in Florida right now, where the only rattling sound I ever heard was mangrove trees quaking in the lazy afternoon rain, and the only smell in the air was the brine of the ocean. Fall in Chicago is beautiful and crisp and all those things my parents brag about, but it's also ghostly. That's really the only word that can describe the feeling here. *Ghostly.*

"Tessa?" Andrew's voice breaks into my observations. I look up, realizing that he and Nina are staring at me, waiting for a reaction. They look excited . . . hopeful. Me? Not so much. But as scared as I am, walking to Inez's grave is the least I can do, considering they were willing to come here for me. To help me. I don't know how I'll ever pay them back.

"Ugh. Fine," I say hesitantly. "But let's be fast."

23

MAP IN HAND, WE TRUDGE IN THE DIRECTION OF Inez's grave. With the exception of the wind rattling the tree limbs, it's silent. Yellow and red leaves whip around as if they're alive, and the air has a bite to it. A chilly and frightening bite.

A flash of lightning brightens up the sky to the east. I know it's the east because I'm finally learning which way Lake Michigan is. Well, that and I've snuck my compass out of my pocket several times to check. Every time Andrew or Nina looks at me, I put it away, desperate to avoid answering questions like *Who carries a compass around with them* and *Why not just use your phone?*

Nina picks up her pace. Her eyes are glued to the

lit screen of her cell phone. "Weather looks bad. Really bad. We can't have more than twenty minutes before this stuff hits us." Her sneakers squeak across the slick black pavement as she leads us deeper into the spread of headstones.

"Twenty minutes?" I ask. "Even if we get to Inez's grave and back to the entrance, we've still got to bike home. We'll never make it."

Nina looks thoughtful. "But we're so close. We can't just walk away now."

She's right. Getting stuck in a storm would suck, but being stuck with a ghost in my house would be much, much worse.

Andrew stops for a moment and I'm going to pull him forward when I see what he's looking at. It's a cluster of small, square houses. They're squat and made of stone and have names etched into them.

"Mausoleums," Nina says in a near-whisper. "They're burial chambers where the dead person is kept in a tomb aboveground."

"Like a crypt," Andrew adds. His hand is tensed tightly around his backpack straps as he stares at the buildings. "I don't think I like those."

Me neither. I look at the accordion gate stretched across a door. Why would they need a gate over it? It's not like the person is going to wake up and try to get out, right? I let out a nervous laugh. I'm never watching another zombie movie again.

We take a left at a fork in the path and I try to remember if this is the way the woman highlighted for us. I think so, but the map is in Nina's pocket. I've just gotten a glimpse of a glass box ahead when thunder shakes the ground and a flash of lightning nearly blinds me.

"That's her!" I scream, pointing at the box. "That's Inez!"

Andrew flicks the hood of his jacket up. "We better do this fast, then, because *that* is going to be horrible!"

I scan the sky. It's black. Andrew is right—as bad as this weather looked on Nina's phone, it's even worse in person. It's also really, really cold. I mean, it didn't exactly feel tropical before, but it wasn't frigid like the sprinkles of rain that are hitting me square in the face, either.

As we creep up to the box, my breath catches in my throat. There's something about standing in front of Inez that's overwhelming. Exciting, but scary at the same time. Seeing a grave with an actual image of the person supposedly buried under it is spooky—much spookier than just seeing a stone nameplate and some random words or dates.

"Wow," Andrew breathes out. I feel his hand on

my arm, probably an attempt to make sure I don't bolt. "This is incredible."

Nina squats down and drags out a notebook, which she perches on her knees. She begins furiously scribbling as my eyes remain fixed on the petite face of the small stone girl in front of us.

"Inez," I whisper. "It's actually you."

My eyes begin at the top of her head and move downward, taking note of everything inside the glass box. She has a young face with adorably full cheeks, and her eyes are soft . . . kind. Her wavy hair is pulled back and she's sitting on what looks like a stone version of a wooden bench, her tiny feet covered by low-heeled slippers. She wears a dress and there's a locket or necklace of some kind hanging from her neck. The object I saw in her hand in the sketchpad back home is a broom . . . no, an umbrella.

An umbrella. My mind spins for a moment, thinking about the legend that a lightning strike killed Inez. Is that why the sculpture is holding an umbrella? I shake off the thought.

"Okay, I think I've got it all." Nina stands up and wipes the drops of rain from her notebook before shoving it in her bag. I've been so absorbed with Inez's statue that I don't even know what she was doing to begin with.

"Got what?" Andrew asks, as if he can read my mind.

"The names and dates of all the graves around Inez's. See how close they are together?"

I hadn't noticed, but Nina is right. There are two smaller gravestones to the left of Inez, and one to the right. They're clumped into a straight line, each of them so close to the next that they're almost touching.

"Only family is buried that way. These other gravestones have to be relatives of whoever is buried here—whether it's Inez or Amos," Nina finishes, sighing.

Andrew's face crinkles up. "Yeah, but if the cemetery people don't really even know who's buried here, they might have buried the wrong family next to them . . . right?"

Nina nods. "Possibly. We won't know until we do a little more research, though."

I'm considering this when a flash of lightning lights up the dark cemetery. For a moment, Inez's face is illuminated . . . nearly glowing. I gasp as an enormous clap of thunder immediately follows the lightning, shaking me to my core. Rain begins falling in fat, white sheets.

"Here we go!" Andrew says, squinting through the rain.

Nina jogs over under the nearest tree and fumbles with the map. Andrew and I follow, shielding our faces from the icy water as best we can. "I think we came from that way, but I just want to make sure," Nina says.

I stare down at the map with her as the storm ramps up around us. Another streak of lightning lights up the sky, and the sound that follows it makes my entire body go cold.

Crying. It cuts through the rain like a knife and settles into my ears. I bite my tongue to keep from screaming.

"Are you okay?" Andrew is asking. I can make out the words, but they're quiet. Distant. He taps my shoulder, then shakes me gently. All I can do is cover my ears as the wailing gets louder.

It's Inez. It has to be.

An unexpected gust of wind whips my coat hood up and over my eyes. It's exactly like the gust that ruffled my hair and pajamas the night Reno started talking in my room—cold and eerie. I yank the hood off my face. That's when I see the footprints. They're shallow and tiny, pressed down around Andrew and me like whoever left the prints was running in circles.

Daring.

Taunting.

Warning.

Andrew gapes at them in horror. He blinks, then looks at me like I might have an explanation, but I don't. I haven't seen anyone else in this cemetery since we got here. Swiveling my head around, I search the headstones. Nothing. I turn to tell Andrew we're okay, that we must have somehow missed those footprints earlier and it's all going to be fine, when I feel them—the fingers. Icy, dead fingers sliding into my open palm . . . tugging me deeper into the darkened cemetery.

24

I HAVE TO GET OUT OF HERE. IT'S THE ONLY thought in my head right now. I let out a primal scream as I shake off the cold flesh still gripping my palm. If the crying and the footprints and the fingers in my hand were Inez, we're in trouble. Not just trouble . . . danger. Whirling back toward the glass box, I notice that Nina has moved closer to the path we followed here and is frozen in place. Her shoes are sinking into the muddy ground and one hand is plastered across her mouth.

"Nina?" I call.

Nothing.

She's angled toward Inez Clarke's glass box, and as my eyes finally find it in the whiteout, I gasp.

Even with the curtain of rain clouding my vision, I can see that the box is one hundred percent, completely *empty*. I stare at the white space where the sculpture was, terrified. The kind eyes and full cheeks are gone. The wavy hair and tiny half-smile . . . gone. The entire sculpture of Inez Clarke is just. Gone.

The warning from the woman at the front office comes back to me. *The statue vanishes during lightning storms.*

A burst of crackles fills my ears and I shudder. She's scared of the lightning. Inez is scared of the lightning and is hiding in this cemetery. My entire body shakes with the thought. I know it doesn't make sense and that my brain is telling me I'm losing it, but right now . . . none of that matters.

"Run!" I screech into the nothing of rain and leaves and howling wind.

Andrew grabs my elbow and tugs me to his side. His hand wraps around mine, his fingers gripping mine urgently. We're sprinting now, racing as fast as we can down the waterlogged path. My mind is spinning. This can't be happening. Inez Clarke's statue did not just vanish in front of our eyes.

"It was empty! Empty!" I yell at him. I can't tell if he hears me over the roar of the storm surrounding us. The wind picks up even more and wet leaves slap my face. Rain hits my body so hard it feels like it's holding me back, trying to keep me in the cemetery.

"This isn't right!" Andrew shouts over the thunder. Lightning flashes nearby and a sharp crack sends a tree limb toppling to the ground.

The crackling seems to weave in and out of the gravestones, following me. "We've got to get back west—toward the entrance!"

West. West. West. I know east now, but in this rain I can't remember where that is, either. It's too dark and we've run in too many circles. Fumbling in my pocket, I try to find my compass but come up empty.

I turn back to see if Nina knows where we are or how far the gate is, but she's not behind us. I tug back on Andrew, fear winding into a tight coil in my belly. "Where is Nina?"

Panic spreads on his face. "What? She was just here!"

She *was* just here. Like, five seconds ago. I search the tangle of headstones as fast as I can, hoping for a glimpse of her blue coat. It isn't there.

"Nina! Niiiinaaaaaaaa!" I scream as loudly as I can, but my voice is no match for the storm roaring around us.

"Nina!" Andrew bellows with me. His blond hair

is matted against his forehead. Water runs in rivers down his cheeks and drips off his chin. He wipes it out of his eyes and points to something up ahead. "Tessa, I see the gate! It's up there!"

I shake my head, tears forming in my eyes. I don't want to head for the gate without Nina, but I don't want to get stuck in the cemetery, either. Turning back to look for her one last time, I'm met with the biggest, most terrifying lightning bolt I've ever seen. It streaks down from the sky, illuminating everything around us for a split second—the frenzy of leaves, the bone-colored headstones, the sinister mausoleums.

But no Nina.

I swivel my head from side to side, then turn a full circle just to be sure. She's gone. Nina is just . . . gone.

25

STANDING OUTSIDE THE CEMETERY GATES, I have to remind myself to breathe. By the time we got back to the entrance, the rain had slowed down to a trickle. The wind died down, too. But Nina . . . Nina was still missing.

Andrew releases my hand and I pull it up into my sleeve quickly. I didn't have time to think about it in the cemetery, about him holding my hand like that, but now I can't help it. It was nice.

He fishes his cell phone out of his pocket and starts pressing buttons.

"What are you doing?" I ask.

"Texting Richie. I don't have Nina's phone number."

"How do you not have that? You've been in school together for years, right?" I ask, panicked. We need to find Nina. My heart slams around in my chest as I think about the bolt of lightning and how she just . . . vanished. Vanished like Inez's statue. Vanished like my mom's watercolors. My stomach rolls.

"I didn't need Nina's phone number before you came along, Tessa!" Andrew snaps. He takes a shaky breath and then looks at me. "I'm sorry. I'm not mad at you. I'm just worried." He leans back and glances through the entrance again. "I've been friends with Richie since first grade. But his sister? I didn't really know her until now."

"Well, number or no number, we have to go look for her," I say, pulling away from his side. "We can't leave her in there alone."

"Too late," Andrew says, his face darkening like the storm that just swept through.

A man in navy blue mechanic's coveralls pulls up in a golf cart. Instead of golf clubs in the back of the cart, he has buckets and a strange collection of yard-work supplies. I watch in horror as he begins dragging the heavy iron gate closed.

"Wait!" I yell, racing toward him. "The sign says the cemetery stays open until three today!"

"Not in inclement weather. Any time we have to clear the paths of tree limbs or debris, we close the gates."

Close the gates? He can't do that. Not until Nina is out. "But our friend is still in there!"

The man looks puzzled. "I'm afraid that's not possible. Our grounds are searched carefully every time we lock up. You two were the last to exit."

"No. Our friend was in there with us! She's about this tall." I hold my hand up to my chin. "And she's twelve."

"Sorry, sweetheart. But she's not in there. We got seven grounds keepers that all run a different route through the cemetery, and at the end my job is to lock up. It's empty in there." He finishes pulling the gate shut and slides a giant lock into place.

I drop my face into my hands and try not to be sick. Bile is bubbling up into my throat.

The golf cart rumbles back to life and I look up to see the man staring at me. His weathered face softens. "Hey. It's okay. Your friend is probably just playing a prank on you two. It wouldn't be the first time in this place."

I want to tell him how un-Nina that would be, but I keep my mouth clamped shut. It doesn't matter what the golf cart man thinks. I know the truth.

Something happened to Nina in that cemetery, and I've got to find her!

The golf cart sputters away, leaving Andrew and me alone. I sink down onto the ground and lean against the wall, not even caring that rainwater is soaking into my jeans.

"Got it!" Andrew tilts his phone down for me to see. It's a text from Richie with Nina's number. Andrew dials the number quickly, then presses the phone to his ear. I don't even have to ask if she answers; his face gives it away.

"I don't get it," I say.

Andrew shakes his head. "Me neither. It went straight to her voice mail. I don't know what to do now."

A ripple of thunder rattles my teeth, and the memory of what we just saw sends fear pulsing through me. "Andrew, that glass box was empty. And Nina disappeared with a flash of lightning. Do you think the ghost did something to her?"

"No. I don't believe in that, Florida. I know you've had some weird stuff going on in your house, but I don't believe for a second that it's a real ghost." He pauses, staring down at his phone as if begging it to ring. "There has to be a rational explanation."

I'm surprised by his answer. I'm even more

surprised that he would agree to come here if he didn't believe in ghosts. Why would he give up soccer and all his other buddies to help me figure this out day after day?

I shake off my surprise and the zillions of questions I want to ask him to focus on one. The most important one. "Then who . . . or what . . . is doing all this? How do you explain what just happened in that cemetery? The crying and the footprints? Nina?"

Andrew shrugs. "I can't answer that yet. But I think there is an explanation. We just need to be patient and find it."

I take one last look through the iron gates at the graveyard. Pressing my face against the cold metal, I scour every patch of headstones that I can see. There's nothing in there that looks like Nina. Nothing alive at all.

26

ANDREW'S PHONE BUZZES JUST AS WE CLIMB off our bikes. He turns it faceup to read the message, then exhales loudly. "Nina is okay. Apparently she freaked out when the lightning struck and took another path back to the entrance."

I'm relieved, but angry. "And she didn't think to tell us?"

"Guess not," Andrew says, tucking his phone back in his pocket. He lifts off his helmet, revealing mussed, damp hair on top, but completely dry hair in the front. Everything that hung out of his helmet sticks up like a peacock's feathers. "We can't really be mad at her for doing the same thing we did, though."

He's right. When I saw that the glass box was

empty, I took off. So did Andrew. I can't blame Nina for running in the other direction. At that point, we all just wanted out. "So we know where Nina is. But what about the footprints?"

Andrew sighs. "You have to admit that maybe it's possible they were already there and we overlooked them. We were looking at the statue, not down at the ground. Right?"

"And the crying?" I continue, panic pulsing in me as I remember the soft wailing that seemed to come from every direction.

"It could have been the wind. You live in the Windy City now, Tess. Sometimes the wind sounds like whistling, sometimes like howling . . . maybe today it sounded like crying." He runs his open palms over his face like he's tired. "Ugh. The one thing I can't explain away is that glass box. I don't know how the statue disappeared like that, but we're going to find out, Florida."

I pause, then take two steps up my front walk. It's now or never. "O-kay. This is it."

Andrew stops in his tracks and looks up at the windows of my house. "You're lucky. My condo building is huge and there's always someone moving in or out. I can't keep them all straight. A private house like this would be so much better."

"Thanks," I answer, pulling the necklace out from under my hoodie. It's the same kind of chain that you'd put a dog tag on, but mine holds my house key. I hated taking off my locket, but wearing both only worked for one day. Too many tangles. With my luck, the second I took this key off the necklace, I'd probably lose it.

"Welcome to the Halloween House." I try to pull off a laugh but sound more like a dying goat.

He snorts and punches me gently in the upper arm. "It's not that bad, and I don't scare easily. Nina, either. Richie, on the other hand . . ."

Wait, Richie and Nina are coming?

Andrew catches my confusion and frowns. "It's okay that I invited them over, right? Richie was worried about his sister, and obviously we have a lot to figure out. I thought four brains would be better than two."

"Yeah, totally. It's great. My parents will be happy to meet you guys, anyway," I say, wilting on the inside. My father will probably break out his violin and ask us to do some kind of weird, folksy sing-along. And Mom—well, who knows? She could be on one of her painting binges where we don't see her for hours at a time, or maybe she'll encourage my friends to let her read tea leaves or something crazy.

Back home my friends were used to Mom and

Dad. If they did something insane—like insist that we all hold hands and meditate like they did the last time Rachel slept over—it wasn't a shock. But here no one knows how different they are yet. How different *we* are. Even though I'm glad Andrew is here, I kinda wish he wouldn't find out.

The house smells like pizza when Andrew and I walk in. Warmth seeps into my clothes as I take off my jacket, heating my chilled skin. As much as I hate this place, those radiator thingies sure can be nice.

"Wow," Andrew says, looking around. His eyes land on the paintings in our living room and he smiles. "Did you make those?"

"Nope. I only work in pastels. My mom is a painter, though. Those are hers."

He slips off his wet shoes and walks over to one—my favorite. It's a heron standing in shallow water with a fiery Florida sunset behind it. "This is really good. Your mom is amazing. She painted back in Orlando, then?"

"Fort Myers," I correct him. I've only been to Orlando twice and it was to celebrate Halloween with Mickey Mouse. Unless you count snack bars and flying carpet rides, there wasn't anything there to paint. "Yeah, that's a scene from a beach that was right by our house. We used to go there all the time."

Andrew must sense the sadness in my tone, because he abandons the painting. Jonah's toys are spread all over the floor like a garage sale exploded in our living room. Fortunately, Reno isn't part of it.

"Tessa! Hey, sweetie, where have you been?" Dad appears in the doorway between the kitchen and the living room. Something red is splattered all over the front of his shirt. He stops when he sees Andrew. "Ah! Well, hello there! You must be a friend of Tessa's."

"I'm Andrew. Nice to meet you." Andrew reaches out to shake my dad's hand. I've never seen a kid do this before, and I almost laugh.

"Andrew is in my homeroom and we have a couple of classes together."

"Fantastic!" Dad says. "So glad you're here. Make yourself at home."

"Um . . . Dad? What is that?" I point a finger toward his shirt. Bringing someone here for the first time is hard enough without Dad walking around looking like a crime-scene photo.

"Pizza sauce. It's Woodward pizza day and you made it just in time!" He does a little dance and his hair bounces around on the top of his head, making me laugh despite my nerves. "Nothing better than homemade pizza for lunch!"

Pizza day is something we did back in Fort Myers a lot. Every weekend, actually. We'd roll out our own dough and make individual pizzas, adding whatever toppings we wanted. It's how I learned that pepperoni and green olives were totally meant to be together. Like pastels and paper.

"Honey, your mom and Jonah walked to the grocery store to get some last-minute toppings for the hot fudge sundaes we're putting together for dessert, but with the storms and all, I'm going to drive to pick them up."

Plan ruined. I can't be here alone with Andrew. The ghost will do something if we're the only ones here.

"It's hardly raining at all now, Dad. And what about us?" I sound whiny, but I can't help it. I'm scared.

"What about you? In two short months, you'll be thirteen, Tessa. We trust you!" He says this with a giant smile as if it's supposed to please me. It does not.

Andrew mouths "free-range" to me and I fight back a laugh. Maybe my parents are part of some new, hip movement here in Chicago and they just don't know it yet.

"Oh, Tessa!" Dad suddenly whirls around, a broad

smile on his face. "Internet got hooked up today!"

I stare at him, excited and disappointed at the same time. I'm finally free to e-mail Rachel any time I want—to tell her all about Chicago and this ghost—but Andrew is here. Plus, Nina and Richie aren't far away. I'll message her later . . . *after* we figure out what Inez is after. She'll understand.

My father slips on a jacket and grabs his keys from the table. "Be right back, guys. Pizzas just came out of the oven, but don't try to cut them yet. They need to cool."

The door slams behind him and I shudder as the giant dead bolt slides back into place. We're alone in here now. Alone with Inez. Or the ghost of Inez. Or Amos. Whatever.

"What was that all about?" Andrew strips off his wet jacket and hangs it on the hook just inside the door.

"Nothing," I say quickly.

Andrew plops down on the couch and kicks out his feet. "Then why did you want your dad to stay here so bad?"

I look at the paintings. The uneven wood floor. The loose brick in the wall I still haven't told him about. Anywhere but at Andrew. "I'm afraid. Afraid for us to be here alone with *her*."

"Who? The ghost?"

Nodding, I look toward the stairwell. "It started the day after we moved in. Mom heard noises, but they were coming from my room. Jonah heard them, too. Again, my room. Then his doll showed up—in *my room.* Twice! I think she's trying to reach me."

I leave out the part about the drawings I found in the wall. I'm pretty sure they're proof of what I'm saying, but I'm not ready to share that theory just yet. Telling Andrew and Nina might get the clues figured out faster than if I do it on my own, but a little voice in my head keeps telling me that isn't what Inez wants. That she left the drawings for *me* to find, and that she wants me to figure them out. I hope I'm not making a mistake by keeping them a secret.

Andrew scratches his head. "Not gonna lie, I feel a little better knowing you weren't acting like a weirdo because of me." He grins that lopsided grin of his and I can't help but smile back. "Maybe we need to start by finding out the connection between her and you," Andrew adds. "Why the ghost is trying to reach you, specifically."

"I thought you didn't believe in ghosts," I tease.

He grins and shrugs. "I guess I'm on the fence about it."

"Ask Nina how far away she is. We might need her."

Nina has more knowledge about Inez than she wants to admit. And right now, I think she's my best shot at unraveling this mess. "Oh! And tell her to bring the book! If we're going to figure out who's buried there and why they're haunting me, we're going to need it."

Andrew starts clicking away at his phone. "Got it. Where's your computer?"

Oh, no. The family computer has always been off-limits to me before—for anything that isn't homework-related, that is. We don't have a television, either. Mom and Dad don't hate technology, really. They just believe there are better things to fill our time with. Now I'm going to have to explain that and look like a complete psycho.

Or am I?

I glance up at the clock, noting that Dad walked out about three minutes ago. With traffic, he should be gone for at least another twenty. Plenty of time to do a little digging on Inez and then erase everything from the computer history. If Nina and Richie get here soon, that is.

Taking a deep breath, I tell myself this is pretty much homework. I'm not really breaking the house rules. Right?

"Upstairs, first door on the right. But the minute they get here, we're going to have to be fast."

27

THE BUZZER RINGS AND ANDREW BEATS ME TO the front door, tossing it open to reveal a waterlogged Nina and an obviously angry Richie. I rush out and throw my arms around Nina's neck.

She tightens up in my grip like she's not used to being hugged, but I don't care. I'm too happy to see her to stop. "Nina! I'm so glad you're okay!"

Pulling back, she gives a half-smile. "Yeah, well . . . me too. I thought we were goners."

"What happened to you guys?" Richie asks, his deep brown eyes landing on me skeptically. "One minute Nina was hogging the bathroom with that stupid water flosser of hers, and the next she's calling me in a panic . . . saying there's a ghost after her."

I take a step back and stare at Nina. "You said that? That a ghost was after you?"

She nods and her cheeks flush pink. "Listen, I didn't just agree to help you with all this because I like you. I mean, I do. But I also think you need help."

"So you agree that what's happening to me isn't just my imagination?" I ask, hope soaring through me for the first time since we left Fort Myers. If Nina believes me—if a girl who is obviously this smart honestly believes I'm being haunted—then I can't be wrong.

Nina nods. The smile that stretches across her face isn't shy or nervous . . . it's happy. Whoever thought a terrifying paranormal experience could bring me such an amazing new friend? And something tells me it's helping her, too. I'm starting to think investigating this ghost is showing Nina how awesome she actually is. Maybe this is a new Nina . . . a more confident one.

Clapping suddenly, Andrew draws a scream from Nina. She looks at me sheepishly and the four of us burst into laughter. "O-kay, so Nina is still a little on edge. Think you guys are up for doing some research on Inez or Amos or whoever seems to be following Tess around?"

Tess. My parents call me that all the time, but it

sounds nicer . . . more sophisticated coming from him. I think I like it.

Richie holds his hands up in the air. "I'm not committing to anything until I know *exactly* what kind of research you're talking about. Is this like the time you asked me to help you figure out if catnip affects humans?"

"No. And how many times do I have to say I'm sorry about that?" Andrew asks, tossing his own hands in the air in annoyance. "We were eight!"

"You dumped it directly into my nostrils! I couldn't breathe right for a week!" Richie shouts.

The image in my head is too funny and I can't help it. I start laughing. "Why would you think catnip would do something to Richie?" I manage to ask between giggles.

Andrew shrugs and fights off a laugh. "I don't know. I just thought it would be great if it did." He paws at the air like a demented cat, and Richie mutters something about not being able to smell anything but mint and leaves for days. Those two. What I wouldn't give to have known them as long as they've known each other.

Nina tips her head toward the kitchen. "Is that where your computer is? We should get working."

"Agreed. But the laptop is actually upstairs.

C'mon." I take Nina's and Richie's jackets and toss them onto the couch. Then I gesture for them to follow me. Even with three friends at my back, I'm still nervous in here. Still feel like I'm being watched.

We march up the steps slowly. Quietly.

"This is the painting," I whisper, stopping in the dim stairwell to show them the image that seems to darken with each hour that passes. The winding tendrils are completely brown and the petals are faded. The smudge in the corner is still there, too, like a warning. *I'm here and I'm not leaving until you give me what I want.*

A creak from the top of the stairs draws my attention and I inhale deeply, preparing myself for the possibility that the crackling is coming. Turning to look at Richie, I notice that his face has gone white. His jaw clenches and unclenches, but he stays silent.

"Are you okay?" I ask him, but I get nothing in return but a curt nod and wide, worried eyes. This guy is more nervous in this house than I am! The creak at the top of the stairs comes again—louder this time, and Richie turns on his heel as if to run.

"Hey! Where do you think you're going?" Andrew grabs the hood of Richie's sweatshirt and pulls him back. "No way are we going to get eaten or maimed by this thing and you're going to just be hanging out at home with that stupid tub of cheese puffs you have hidden under your bed."

"Shut up about my cheese puffs!" Richie hisses, scrambling out of Andrew's grip. "And for the record, I'm not scared. I just don't think I have anything to add here."

Andrew smirks. Fortunately, though, he's got the good sense to stay quiet. Richie looks like he's about to black out and I'm positive Andrew's sarcasm is not going to help.

A muted thump travels down the stairs and I rub at my arms, trying uselessly to make the goose bumps go away. "I would say that's nothing, but . . ."

"But that would obviously be a lie," Andrew finishes. His eyes land on mine and he winks. "C'mon, Florida. *No fear.* This ghost obviously doesn't want to hurt you, or she would have done it already. So let's just ignore the sounds, get the computer, and figure out who's buried in that cemetery."

Nina slips a tiny camera out of her pocket and begins fitting it into a clear plastic case. Then she attaches the case to some kind of strap and slips it onto her head. The camera rests against her forehead, and its giant eye stares at me.

"What the . . . are you videoing?" I ask.

"Abso-freaking-lutely. If there is some kind of

presence in your house, I want to catch it on this!" She gently taps the camera, which I now notice says HERO on the front. The musty lightbulb in my brain turns on. It's a GoPro. Tons of kids had them back in Florida for surfing and snorkeling and fishing on the beach.

I guess I didn't realize that city kids had anything as interesting to record.

Nina turns and lets her camera fully take in the painting before we continue moving up. Rounding the banister at the top, I leap into the center of the hallway and turn a full circle.

Crickets.

"What are you doing?" Andrew laughs. His eyes are crinkled up by the giant smile that's plastered onto his face. "Are you trying to surprise the ghost? Because I'm not sure that's how it works . . ."

"Oh, shut up. How would you know the way it works, anyway? Hmmm? Do *you* have an artistically talented ghost in your house?" I stop speaking suddenly. The idea is so simple I don't know how I didn't think of it before. "Wait! Maybe that's it!"

Andrew stops laughing and tips his head to the side in confusion. "What's it?"

"The drawings!" I fling my door open, no longer worried about what might be on the other side. "I never thought about it before, but if this ghost is the ghost of Inez Clarke, why is she trying so hard to reach me through drawings?"

He thinks on this for a moment, his eyes suddenly lighting up like fireworks on the Fourth of July. "Because you like to draw?"

"Bingo!" I yell. Reaching into my desk, I pull out the sketchpad with the glass box drawn in it. I hold the image up. Andrew and Nina gasp in unison.

"Whoa! That's the statue!" Nina pulls the sketchpad from my hands and holds it up for her camera. "It's so obviously the exact same one!"

I nod enthusiastically. Now that I've seen the real tombstone, I completely believe that Inez Clarke is behind the creepshow going on in my house. The drawings. The crying and the rattling doorknob. Reno.

I look at the corner Reno appeared in that night, grateful to see it's empty.

"Look. This is a good pastel drawing. A great one, actually."

Richie crosses the room in a few short strides and stares down at it. I hadn't noticed before, but he came from the window. Something tells me he was looking out and wishing he wasn't stuck in this place. Poor guy looks like he's actually *seen* a ghost, instead of just hearing about one.

"This is really good, Tessa. And you have no idea who did it?" he asks.

"None. Only that they keep adding to it. Almost daily there's more drawn, but I never see signs that anyone has been in here."

Andrew narrows his eyes at the image, then looks up at me. "Why isn't there a face, though? It's like it's only an outline."

"Exactly! Only a real pastel artist starts with an outline like this." I'm so excited that I'm almost screaming. Yet Andrew still looks . . . lost.

"I'm saying maybe that's the connection!" I tell myself to slow down before I lose Andrew completely. "Let's start at the beginning. It seems like this ghost is a girl—Inez. It also seems like maybe she liked to draw and that's why she's haunting me!" I remember about the crying I heard in the hallway and how it didn't sound like Jonah. It definitely sounded like a girl.

Maybe the graveyard records have it all wrong. Maybe Inez Clarke isn't the one who didn't exist. After all, what proof do we have that Amos Briggs ever existed? None.

Andrew stays perfectly still for a minute, deep in thought. His eyes flick back and forth between the drawing and me; then he exhales. "Smart, Tessa. That could be it!"

"I don't know," Nina says. Her voice sounds skeptical. "She was only six when she died. Could a six-year-old be this good at drawing?"

She has a point. But outlines *are* the very first thing that an artist who works with pastels learns. And the other drawings I found—the secret ones from behind the brick—are pretty rough. If I can connect those to Inez somehow, maybe this all makes more sense than we thought. It's possible Inez was just learning to draw and that's why the images aren't all complete.

"What other connection is there?" Andrew asks Nina. "Tessa's not from Chicago, she's not dead . . ."

I punch him in the arm. "That was mean. And she could be listening!"

"Fine." He looks up at my ceiling. "I didn't mean it, Inez."

I make a *tsk*ing sound at him. "Better hope she forgives you. Unless you want her following you home, that is."

"I'd rather stuff catnip in *my* nose," Andrew admits sheepishly.

This time it's my turn to laugh at him. And I do. Hard.

Richie and Nina laugh along with me, and for a moment I forget why we're here. That there's something ominous in my new house and I've recruited my only friends in this entire city to help me solve it.

It might not be the start I was hoping for here in Chicago, but it isn't the end of my life, either. And Inez . . . if she is the one haunting me, she'd better watch out, because thanks to these guys, I'm on her trail.

28

"HEY—WHAT'S THIS?" NINA STOOPS DOWN ON the opposite side of my bed. I walk over to her, my blood going cold at the sight. A moving box. It's sitting right next to my bedside table and is labeled with my mother's name.

Her supplies.

"Oh my god," I whisper. "My mom was looking for these. They disappeared from our kitchen right after we moved in."

Nina tightens the strap of her camera. It makes her brown hair stick out even more than it did when she first put it on. "I'm guessing this wasn't here earlier today?"

I shake my head grimly, then kneel down and lift

the lid to be sure. It's Mom's good set of watercolors. I'm willing to bet Mom has no idea they're in here. I didn't even know they were in here! That's because someone . . . or something . . . wanted *me* to get the message first. But what is the message? That the ghost can get into my room? The ghost already proved that by drawing in my sketchpad, so why go a step further? Why keep tormenting me?

Richie looks at me nervously as he begins to fidget with the zipper of his hooded sweatshirt. "And she wouldn't have brought them in here after you left for the day? Like, maybe stuck them in your room so she could have more space to unpack other stuff?"

"Nope." It's a good guess, but no way. Mom is very protective of her art supplies, just like I am about my pastels. There's no good explanation for why they're in here. Nina walks the edges of my room, quietly documenting everything she sees for the big black eye of her camera. I hope that thing catches something we don't, because right now I feel completely outmatched.

Black clouds roll across the endless gray, blanketing my room in darkness. I flip on my reading light and shoot Richie a look I hope is comforting. The wind picks up, and the massive tree in my front yard shimmies back and forth like it's being shaken by invisible hands. Maybe it is.

"I have a bad feeling about this," Richie whispers, his eyes glued to the menacing sky. "It had finally calmed down out there after the storm earlier. No wind. Nothing. And now it looks like a zombie apocalypse is coming. *Again*."

Nina walks over to the window and surveys the wind and clouds for herself, muttering something that sounds like "weather anomalies" for her camera. Then she turns back to face me with a serious look in her eyes. "This seems to be a theme, doesn't it? Stormy weather when the topic of Inez comes up?"

"Ahhh, I don't know if we can connect those two things, though," Andrew says, pulling back my curtains to reveal more of the window. "Fall is always weird here. Sometimes it still feels like summer and other times—" A sharp crack of thunder rings through the room, interrupting him.

The four of us stay silent as the air in the house grows heavy. My reading lamp flickers on and off, the bulb humming with an energy I wished I'd never have to feel again. It's her. The ghost. It has to be.

A soft wailing fills my room. It's so quiet I almost miss it. But I know Andrew, Nina, and Richie don't.

The look of utter horror on their faces tells me they hear it.

Is it . . . is it coming from under my bed? I close my eyes and try to breathe deeply. Visions of Reno hiding just beyond my dust ruffle dance behind my eyelids and I try to ignore them. *He's just a doll. He's just a doll. He's just a doll.*

Nina adjusts the camera on her forehead with trembling fingers and gives me a small nod.

Slowly, I slide down onto the floor and lift the dust ruffle. My hands are shaking so hard I can barely hang on to the lacy fabric. I force myself to look underneath, exhaling a breath of relief. It's empty. I can take wind and thunder and rain—even crying—but I *cannot* take Reno. If he shows up right now, I'm outta here.

"Tessa, what are you looking for?" Richie has moved to my door and has one hand tensed on the doorknob. "And what is that sound? Tell me it's your little brother!"

There's still zero color in Richie's face. A few small pinpricks of sweat shine on his forehead and his hand is gripping the doorknob so tightly that his knuckles are white. Guilt crushes me. Richie is nice, and despite the fact that he's tall and looks more like he's in high school than in seventh grade, that doesn't mean I should expect him to be any braver than us.

"My mom said the plumbing is weird in these old houses," I lie. "It was probably just the pipes whining."

Richie looks unconvinced. "And you were looking under the bed *because* . . ."

"I was just thinking maybe I left something we might need under there, is all." I could tell him I was looking for a possessed ventriloquist dummy, but why? Expecting Richie to investigate this with us is no different than my parents expecting me to move here and love it. Things like that take time. And sometimes . . . sometimes they never come.

A bolt of lightning streaks from the sky and appears to go straight down to the city's core. The thunder that follows is deep and makes the glass in my window shake. The wailing goes silent, but the entire house buzzes with a dark energy. *Her* energy.

Inez is here. She's here and she wants something from me. In my mind I again run through the drawings I found behind the brick, desperate to make sense of them. If I could just understand her clues, maybe I'd be able to figure out what she wants. Bedroom. Music box. Bedroom. Music box. Bedroom. Music box . . . *I. B.* I'm lost. Completely lost.

Richie cranes his neck as if he's listening for the

crying to return. His eyes are darting around, landing on nothing for more than a split second before moving again. I remember what Andrew said about him earlier and smile. Twins or not, he and Nina are very different people, and that's okay. I know what I need to do.

"Hey, don't you have something today? Soccer?"

Richie nods. "Yeah, it's starting in twenty minutes." He looks back out the window to the swirling torment outside. "Practice will probably be inside now, thanks to this stupid storm."

"You should call your mom or dad and have them pick you up so you aren't late," I say, hoping he gets the hint. It's like the time my mom told me I needed to take a break from my pastels—just a day or two. I'd been making myself crazy over this one image, erasing and starting over, erasing and starting over. I'd done it so many times I was in tears, and although I couldn't see my problem, Mom could. I just needed to get away from the pressure I was putting on myself. Maybe Richie needs an out, too.

"Maybe. Yeah, that might be a good idea. You coming?" Richie looks at Andrew expectantly.

"Nah. Coach thinks I'm sick, so you can do me a favor and back me up. Tell him I'm puking or something," Andrew says, following up with an obviously fake cough and a wicked little grin.

Richie gives him a look, something I'd love to decode, and then tosses me a smile. Guy isn't bad-looking when he's not scowling. Or terrified. "All right, then. I'll catch you guys later. Sorry I can't stay and help, Tessa. The soccer thing . . ." He trails off and I nod as if I'm disappointed but understand. Hopefully he buys it.

He disappears through my door and even though there's a storm raging, I feel warm inside. It's like my mom said . . . sometimes people won't let themselves off the hook and you need to do it for them. I'm glad I did that for Richie.

29

"THAT WAS NICE OF YOU, FLORIDA," ANDREW SAYS, winking. It's my favorite thing he does, that wink, but right now I'm grateful he doesn't know that.

"I don't know what you're talking about," I say, fighting off a smile.

Nina lifts the camera off her head and looks down at the floor for a moment. "He's scared of this stuff. He'll never admit it, but he is. That's why I try not to get mad at him for making fun of my cemetery and ghost research. I think he does it because it makes him nervous."

"Well, it makes me nervous, too. The only difference is that I don't have a choice." My reading lamp flickers again and the small hairs on the back of my neck rise. The electricity Inez creates is pulsing just under my skin again. She's trying to tell me something. I just don't know what.

I reach back and rub my neck, trying to ease the feeling. If Andrew and Nina can feel it, too, they sure don't show it.

Nina gasps and we turn to look at her. Her face is tilted down toward the screen of her camera. "Oh . . . holy . . . what in the . . ."

This can't be good. Andrew and I crowd around her, craning our necks to see the small screen. She hits the pause button and turns to look back at us, her eyes wild and frightened.

"I'm going to rewind this so you can see it. But . . . Tessa, I don't want you to panic, okay?"

Panic? Why would I panic? It's not like a ghost has made a ventriloquist dummy cry actual tears, and left mysterious drawings hidden inside my wall, and held my hand in a graveyard, or anything.

"*Pffft.* I'm fine. Show me."

With a few more taps, she's rewound the video she just took and begins playing it back in slow motion. It begins with me crouching down and searching underneath my bed. Yes, I remember doing that. The footage rolls by slowly. I watch myself straighten back up, and in that instant, a flash of lightning brightens the entire room.

"There!" Nina screams, her index finger jabbing frantically at the mirror over my dresser in the video. I squint hard and gasp as I finally see what got her so wound up.

It's a face. A small . . . very young . . . very little-girlish face is reflected in the mirror. I bring a hand to my mouth to keep horrible four-letter words from spilling out. Unlike the soft smile on the statue of Inez Clarke, this face is dark. Frightening. Pitch-black eyes like the night are set against porcelain skin, and her lips are pale. She doesn't look happy. She doesn't look alive.

"Oh my god," I say, pushing the camera away. I don't want to see it anymore. I don't *need* to see it anymore because the image of that ghostly face is going to be forever burned into my mind. My entire body trembles with the thought that she was in here with me. *With us.*

Andrew scrunches up his face and sits down on my bed. "I don't get it. There was no one in this room with us. No one."

"There was no one in the cemetery with us, either. Remember? The footprints?" I remind him.

"Footprints?" Nina asks. "What are you talking about?"

"Right before the statue disappeared, there was this strong breeze. It blew my hood up over my face so I couldn't see, but when I pulled it back off and looked around, there were footprints in the ground. Little footprints. They weren't there before, Nina. We would have seen them."

Nina scribbles frantically in her journal. "I can't believe you guys forgot to tell me this!"

"They could have been there before we arrived," Andrew asserts. But this time he doesn't sound convinced. "And about this—" He waves his hand at Nina's camera. "A reflection doesn't happen unless there's someone in front of the mirror to create it."

"That can't be true. I just showed you evidence that it isn't," Nina responds flatly. Instead of being afraid, she sounds determined. "Was that the first time you've seen her, Tessa?"

I nod numbly. I've seen *signs* of her, but I've never seen Inez herself. Until today.

Andrew laughs nervously. "Well, I'm a believer now. And I think she's starting to get impatient with us."

"Paranormal activity *can* become extreme," Nina says. "There are documented cases of fires starting on their own and houses caving in on themselves."

Houses caving in on themselves? I've never gotten

the feeling that the ghost haunting me is that angry, but maybe I'm wrong. Either way, I don't want to test her.

The front door slams, sucking the air right out of my lungs. Mom and Dad are back, and my computer-napping chance is gone.

"Ugh. Oh, no." I press the heels of my palms into my eyes until I see spots. "They're back. My parents are back."

Nina pats my shoulder. "Hey—it's all good. I was kinda excited to meet them anyway."

"Her dad's cool," Andrew says. "Covered in pizza sauce, but cool."

I'd laugh if I weren't so frustrated. "It's not that. It's just—" The deep, somber notes of my dad's violin drift up the stairwell, interrupting me. For the first time I can remember, it isn't calming.

"Are you going to tell them about this?" Andrew says, nudging my door open a bit farther with his foot. The sound of the strings intensifies and my head is suddenly killing me.

"Tessa? Is something wrong?" Nina asks, unzipping her GoPro case to put the camera away. Thank goodness. If I'm about to have some kind of weird nervous breakdown, I don't want it to be caught on video.

"No. Well, maybe. But you have to promise you guys won't think I'm weird or anything if I tell you," I say. They have to understand this. I need them to.

Andrew snorts loudly and jabs a finger out toward her. "She's got a camera strapped to her head, Tessa. And you're worried that *you* might look weird?"

Nina reaches to slap him, but he slides away quickly, laughing. I wish I could laugh with them. It's just too difficult right now. I swallow hard and get ready to tell them how backward the Woodward family really is.

"I can't tell my parents about this because they're a little . . . ahh . . . laid-back about stuff. They won't take it very seriously."

"Have you tried?" Andrew asks.

I shake my head. "No. They just have a lot of other stuff going on and . . ." I trail off, trying to decide how exactly I want to explain this to them. "I guess I want to solve this myself. With you guys. For some reason, I just feel like that's what's supposed to happen."

"Then trust your heart," Nina says quietly. "We won't tell them anything yet, but if things get worse or the ghost starts hurting you . . ."

"You'll have to tell them. No questions asked," Andrew finishes for her. His expression is pained, and I can't help but wonder if he's worried for me.

I close my eyes and let Dad's violin fill my ears. It's time to get to the bottom of things, but there's no way to do it unless I'm honest with them. And they deserve it.

"One more thing—I don't have a laptop. Or a phone," I blurt out. Embarrassment floods me and I look down at the worn rug on my floor. It's got gnarled edges and is losing its color.

"O-kay. So why did you say we could come up here to use the computer?" Andrew asks. His tone isn't sarcastic or mean. It's just . . . Andrew.

I sigh. "We do have a family computer, but it's only used for paying bills and homework and stuff like that. And now that my parents are back, I don't have a chance of using it without them noticing. I'm sorry, guys."

"What are you sorry about?" Andrew asks. "That you don't have your own computer, or that you tried to hide it from us?"

"I wasn't hiding it. Not exactly."

Nina waggles her eyebrows at me. "Right. And Andrew doesn't like Doritos."

"Fine," I laugh. "I'm sorry I don't have my own computer, *and* I'm sorry I tried to hide it. I should have known I can't hide anything from you lunatics."

"No, you should have known you don't *need* to hide anything from us lunatics," Andrew corrects, a sympathetic smile on his face. "Got it?"

"Got it."

Good! Because we've got work to do!" Andrew spins me toward my mirrored closet door. My startled reflection stares back at me. "Look there. That's the face of a girl who's going to solve the biggest ghost mystery Chicago has ever seen—computer or no computer!" He claps me on the shoulder and scoops up his backpack.

"Where are we going?" I ask, scrambling for my shoes and jacket.

Andrew smirks. "You'll see."

I snatch a sheet of paper out of my drawer and scribble out a note to Mom about her supplies. Knowing her, she's probably taking Jonah to his room to get him changed into dry clothes after the rain. I'll just drop this on the counter when she's not looking so she'll find it later and stop worrying. Doing it now might get us stuck here—with the adventure jar and Reno—for the night, and I can't afford that. Not when it feels like we're so close to some answers.

30

"WE HAVE TO BE FAST HERE. MY PARENTS . . . they think I'm at my neighbor's house, and once it gets dark, they'll expect me home," Nina pants out. She brushes a string of damp brown hair out of her eyes.

Andrew scowls. "It's only two o'clock, Nina. How long do you think this is going to take?"

"I don't know!" She huffs. "I kind of lose track of time when I'm researching this kind of stuff."

Because she loves it. Andrew and me? Yeah, we're just hoping to survive.

"If everything goes according to plan, we'll find what we need and get out of here in less than an hour," Andrew says, snaking a lock around his bike.

I don't say it, but the idea of an entire hour of

ghost research makes my stomach churn. I wish I could be more like Nina right now. She's curious, not petrified. "Richie is still at practice, right?"

"Yup. This will be easier without him," Nina says, smirking as she lifts off her bike helmet. "It's called coimetrophobia, in case you're wondering."

"Coimetro-what?" Andrew asks.

"Coimetrophobia. Fear of cemeteries. I think Richie has it." She pauses thoughtfully for a moment. "He *hates* graveyards and talk about dead people and ghosts . . . but mostly the graveyards."

If Nina is right and her brother is afraid of cemeteries, he definitely wouldn't have liked our trip to Graceland. It still bothers me. The way the wind and rain picked up like that, flying into our eyes so we couldn't find the way out. The lightning and the crinkle of wet leaves under our feet as we raced to escape. The empty glass box.

If the ghost of Inez Clarke is following me, she was definitely there with us. And I don't think she wanted me to leave.

"Hey! Florida! Get with it." Andrew is holding the door open for me. I love libraries most of the time, but today I'm nervous. Once we get access to their computers and start digging around, there's no telling what we might find.

* * *

We've read every single page of this website on Graceland ghosts and have found nothing new. Nothing different. All the same old ghost legend. And absolutely none of it seems right.

Inez Clarke died from a lightning strike. Inez Clarke never existed. A little boy is buried under the statue. Amos Briggs. Lightning strike. Disappearing statue. Crying in the graveyard. Amos Briggs. Never existed.

The words blur into a blackened mess in front of me. I let my head fall back in exhaustion, wishing I could get just one good night's sleep. We have to be missing something.

Nina puffs the bangs out of her eyes. "I don't get it. This article claims that Inez never existed and that the statue was just an advertisement for a local sculptor. Andrew Gagel."

"Of course. Because why shouldn't things get even weirder? His name just had to be Andrew, didn't it?" Andrew groans.

The connections *are* a bit creepy, but I don't tell him that. "Just a coincidence. And I don't buy into that theory at all. That would have been a really complicated advertisement. The guy had to use a ton of materials to make that thing. And a lot of time!"

"I'm just telling you what this says. Maybe with

no television and Internet there wasn't any other way for him to get new clients or something?"

Andrew is shaking his head. "That would explain why neither Inez Clarke nor Amos Briggs shows up in the census at the time, though. If he made them up for his ad—"

"Nope, there's still a problem," I say, pointing to the article up on my screen. I bring the cursor across a chunk of text to highlight it for them. "Mary Clarke existed. She was a real person in the Chicago census at that time and her name is listed just below Inez's on the gravestone, remember?"

I can't imagine anyone in their right mind letting someone put their name on a realistic-looking gravestone no matter how much that dude needed the business. It's spooky. And morbid.

Nina looks perplexed. "Why would he make up two names and then randomly choose one real person to etch into that tombstone?" She rubs her temples for a moment and then refocuses on me. "I mean, that would be like me making a gravestone and putting Andrew's name on it."

"Hey!" Andrew yelps. "Stop using me for examples if they're going to be all freaky and stuff." He looks back at his screen, muttering something under his breath about death not being funny.

I'd laugh at him, but I kinda agree. Until I figure out what the ghost in my house wants, you won't catch me joking around about it. The face in the mirror surfaces in my mind and I tremble again. How am I ever going to sleep knowing she's there? Watching me?

Andrew's phone vibrates against the wooden table. He slides it toward him and reads the text. A deep sigh follows.

"Everything okay?" I ask. Hopefully it isn't his mom or something. I've seen the free-range half of him, but it would be a bad time for the "you're grounded" half to make an appearance.

"Yeah. It's all good. That was Cass. She was wondering where we are."

Nina makes a face, then buries her nose in the computer screen. I would, too, if I were her, because something tells me this conversation isn't going to be fun.

"By 'we' she meant you and Nina, though, right?" I ask.

"I don't know."

"Yes, you do."

Andrew's eyes find mine. They're apologetic. "I'm going to figure out what's going on with her, Florida. I promise."

I've had enough. Enough of this girl and her drama. "Maybe I don't want you to. Maybe I don't even want to be her friend at this point."

I know I sound petty and childish, but I don't care. I'm mad. Cassidy is ruining her friendship with them but somehow making me feel like I'm to blame.

"I think you do, though. You're nice, Tessa. Nice people want to be friends with everyone."

He's not wrong. Other than Billy Neimeyer—a boy who poured glue into a Dixie cup and tried to convince me it was milk in second grade—I can't remember ever having a real enemy. Is that what Cassidy is? An enemy? The thought makes me queasy.

"Plus, you and Cass have a lot in common."

"We have *nothing* in common, Andrew. Nothing."

He holds a hand up. "Before you go looking for a sharp object, just listen. Cassidy is really creative. She's got such a good imagination that the drama teacher at school lets her tell all the spooky stories to the younger kids at Halloween. She's thoughtful, too."

I shoot him a skeptical look.

"Well, she's usually thoughtful, anyway."

I fold my arms over my chest, hoping I look unimpressed. I want Andrew to believe that hearing him say nice things about Cassidy doesn't bother me, but it does. I remember the hate in her eyes the last time we saw each other, the way she looked directly at me and then walked away even though Nina was begging her to stay. It made me feel terrible.

"If she's so great, why is she treating you guys like this? Is it just because she doesn't like me?" I ask.

Andrew shakes his head grimly. "Nah. I don't think so. Cassidy *is* great, but she's kind of private sometimes. Like this one time in fifth grade she didn't show up for school three days in a row. Me, Nina, and Richie all called her—a bunch—but her mom just kept saying she was in bed, *recovering,* and that she'd call us when she was ready."

"Recovering from what?"

"Surgery. We found out a week later that she had her appendix taken out."

I think about this for a minute, confused. If I needed to have surgery, I'd definitely tell my friends. Especially if I was going to miss school. "I don't understand why she kept it from you guys."

Andrew shrugs. "Like I said . . . private."

Huh. I don't want to admit that I know someone like this, but I do. Rachel. Rachel is my best friend in the world, but she's also the most private person I know. Probably why she wasn't impressed that I told my dentist about her crush on Warner Higgins.

"Wow," Nina whispers. "I know you guys are in

the middle of, um . . . something, but you gotta look at this."

I swivel around to face her. Talking about anything other than Cassidy—graveyards included—sounds great. I blink at Nina's computer screen, hoping my brain can switch gears. "What? Did you find something about Inez?"

Nina nods. "I really should have looked into her legend sooner."

"No kidding," I retort.

She gives me a side-eye. "No, I'm serious. This stuff is fascinating." Angling her screen so that Andrew and I can see, she taps her index finger on a blurry white image. "This is the travel blog of some old woman who visited a bunch of haunted locations in the Midwest last year. This photo was taken at Graceland."

I squint at the white blur, confused. "Is that fog?"

Andrew scrunches up his face, then shakes his head at me. "I think it's a headstone. See the edges of it there in the background?"

I do see the edges. Problem is, the white blur is transparent. Like something is hovering in front of the grave. My skin crawls. "Nina . . . what does the blog say that is?"

Nina purses her lips, confirming my fear. Whoever took that picture says it was a ghost. *Inez's ghost.*

"No way," Andrew breathes out, smashing his face impossibly close to the screen. "It's probably just some sort of camera malfunction. That stuff happens all the time, right?"

"Not really," Nina answers. She flips a few pages in her notebook and pauses on the one titled "Graceland Trip." "Remember how I wrote down the names of all the graves around Inez's? Well, I even copied down the ones several feet away."

"Why?" I ask. My heart beats wildly, so loudly I'm afraid the librarian might come over and ask me to leave because she can hear it.

Nina rolls her shoulders. "I thought we might need them, and I was right. If you look at this picture closely"—she uses the cursor to make the image bigger—"there! See it?"

"'Frank Philmer.'" Andrew reads the name on the grave. "Who in the heck is Frank Philmer?"

Nina waves her hand in the air. "It doesn't matter who Frank Philmer is! What matters is that the picture of this ghostly *thing* was taken very close to Inez's grave. Three headstones down, to be exact."

I scan the names on her notebook paper, impressed. Sure enough, she wrote down everything she observed this morning, down to the shape of the headstones. "So you think that is an actual picture of Inez's ghost?"

"I think it could be. Listen to this." Nina turns the screen back toward herself enough to whisper-read aloud. "'As soon as the apparition appeared, I heard a wailing. The soft wailing of a young girl. I felt her icy breath on my neck as I stood there, paralyzed with fear. Had it not been for the storm that blew in and ended my visit to Graceland, I might have passed out cold among the headstones.'"

The soft wailing of a young girl. Icy breath on her neck. Storm. My eyes drift back to the blurry white spot in the picture. The white blur *was* Inez. It had to be.

31

THE SUN IS LOWER IN THE SKY, BLINDING US as we open the doors of the library to step out. I shield my eyes, struggling to see anything in the piercing light. "I guess the weather cleared up. How long were we in there, anyway?"

"About an hour, and no kidding. This is crazy," Nina says, stumbling over a crack in the sidewalk. "One minute it looks like a tornado is coming and the next, it's clear and beautiful. It even feels warmer out here, don't you think?"

Andrew looks at me and nods. "Think it's because she's happier?"

I'm about to ask who when I realize that would be a dumb question. Of course he means Inez. I think on it for a minute. Maybe she is happier. Maybe that's why the weather is so nice now. Or maybe we're both completely crazy for thinking a ghost can control the weather.

"Hey—you didn't see anything online about music boxes when you were researching Inez, did you?" I ask Nina.

"Music boxes? No. Why?"

"No reason," I answer, disappointed. I tell myself that the second I have some time alone, I'm going to dig the drawings out from where I hid them and figure out what they mean. The *I. B.* on the back is making me crazy. It can't be initials because—hello, Inez *Clarke.* So what is it?

Nina slides her camera over her forehead again and starts surveying the area. Andrew just shakes his head.

"What are you doing now? Filming the outside of the library?" I laugh. Nina sure does have a lot going on in that brain of hers.

"Hey—after what we saw in your room, I want to document *everything.* At the cemetery, I didn't have my camera, and think how much I probably missed."

"Hey! What are you guys doing here?" Richie interrupts, pulling up on his bike. He's smiling like the cat that ate the canary. "Don't tell me you're still digging around on that ghost crap. It's been two hours!"

Nina flicks off the power button on her camera and levels a glare in his direction. "Don't start with me, Richie. Just because Tessa here gave you an excuse to—"

"Whoa, whoa." I clamp a hand over her mouth to shut her up. I don't need Nina telling Richie that I knew he was scared earlier and that's why I encouraged him to leave. "I didn't do anything but remind him about soccer. That's all."

Richie looks from me to Nina. There's a questioning expression on his face.

I shrug. "I didn't play any competitive sports back in Florida, but I figure they're pretty serious about practices. Knucklehead here will probably have a lot to catch up on later." I toss a thumb out toward Andrew, who shoots me a slightly offended look.

"Yeah . . . yeah, they really are. But soccer was great today! I scored the winning goal for our team!"

Andrew's jaw drops. "You what? You were playing forward? I'm a forward! You're a defender!"

Richie puffs out his chest. "Not today. Today I got to show my stuff, since you were gone. I can't be sure, but I think Coach was pretty impressed!"

I can practically hear the anger vibrating off Andrew. This sucks. I didn't expect him to skip practice today and I definitely didn't ask him to. Now he's missed something important because of me.

Putting a hand on his shoulder, I try for a smile. "I'm sorry you weren't there. It's my fault."

"Not your fault, Florida," he spits out. "It's my own. I just wanted to help you with this. Since I never miss practices, I thought it wouldn't be a problem."

"Should we go talk to your coach? I could make something up, tell him my dog ran away or—" Nina starts.

Richie cuts her off before Andrew has a chance to answer. "Number one, we don't have a dog. Number two, Coach won't care. Some of the kids we play with haven't been able to go on a real vacation with their parents in years because of this team." Richie's eyes glint mischievously in the rapidly setting sun. "Though now that he's found something as interesting as soccer, I'm not sure Andrew really cares."

With Richie's comment, Andrew's eyes skip to mine, and they're so bright. So blue. I look away.

Of course he cares. Andrew loves soccer. That's what they keep telling me, anyway. Obviously Richie is talking about the ghost research being more interesting to Andrew than soccer. He's not talking about me. No, that would be crazypants.

"Well, thank you," I whisper, unsure of what else

to say. There really isn't a way to thank him for what he's given up. "But I don't want you missing any more, okay? Not for this."

"Don't worry," he says, pulling out a baseball cap and putting it on. "I've worked my butt off on that team for three years now. A few missed practices won't change that."

I shake my head at him. Andrew skipping practices makes me feel bad, but something about it also makes me feel a little special. Although I didn't agree with my parents at first, I'm beginning to think they're right about something: family should support each other—friends, too. No one should give up the things they love because they think they have to. Including Andrew.

"No. No more missing practice. Promise?"

Andrew goes silent for a minute. His face is frozen in an expression that lands somewhere between shocked and pleased. "Whatever you say, Florida. But remember we still have a ton of stuff to figure out. Inez versus Amos, lightning strike, the empty case."

The empty case! I'd almost forgotten about that. Inez was in the box one minute and the next, poof! She'd vanished.

"What empty case?" Richie asks.

I start to wave him off, but the look on Andrew's face is quietly warning for some reason. Does he *want* me to talk ghosts with Richie? Richie is his best friend—why doesn't Andrew seem worried that he might get spooked again?

"Ahhh . . . I'm sure there's a rational explanation for it. No worries," I say, hoping to make it sound less scary.

"For a box that had a statue in it one minute and was totally empty the next?" Andrew asks exaggeratedly. "No way."

I mouth "Shut up" at him, but he just smiles at me. His lips turn up at the edges just enough to tell me he knows exactly what he's doing.

Richie looks thoughtful. He pushes the kickstand down on his bike and sits on the stoop. "How did it happen? Like, really fast or over some time?"

Nina fumbles around in her bag for a moment and pulls out the journal she had at the graveyard. "I wrote the time down when we went in. I didn't write the time down when I walked back through the gates, well . . . because of the whole storm and panic and all, but I know what time it was when I looked at my phone a couple of blocks away."

"You wrote the time down when you went in?" Richie asks, one eyebrow raised.

She nods. "Yeah. I didn't know if we'd need it, but I'm glad I did. A good researcher takes detailed notes." Nina runs her finger down the lines on her paper, stopping abruptly. "Aha! Here it is! We walked into the lobby at nine-oh-three. And I checked my phone again at ten-oh-five."

"We talked to the woman in the front lobby for a bit, but then we walked to the grave site. Nina probably documented things for at least fifteen or twenty minutes while we looked at the grave and just talked," Andrew chimes in.

Richie nods. "I think I got it. And the weather was stormy the whole time, or no?"

"No." I speak up, still confused as to why Richie is suddenly playing Sherlock Holmes. "It was cloudy, but it wasn't raining when we got there. Then it got really cold and the storm moved in."

"Got cold, huh?" Richie asks.

"Really cold," I clarify. I don't want to scare Ritchie, but if he's going to ask for the facts, I at least want them to be the right ones. "The woman in the lobby told us that legend claims Inez disappears from her case in lightning storms because she's afraid of the lightning. I would have told you that's ridiculous a week ago, but now . . ."

Richie's eyes move down to the book in Nina's hand and then back to me.

Nina folds her journal back up and crams it into

her bag, then tugs on his sleeve. "Hey, we better get home. I'll keep thinking on this, and if I come up with anything new, I'll call you guys."

"Call Andrew," I remind her. "I have that whole no-phone thing going on."

"Right. See you guys Monday. Sunday is supposed to be kind of chill in our house, so my parents don't really like us to make plans," Nina says, sliding the camera back off her forehead.

I nod and smile. Tomorrow is supposed to be family day in my house, too. But how are we supposed to enjoy it with Inez around? I can't stand the thought of the crackling coming back. Turning to look at Andrew, I notice he's staring at me.

"Hey, stop worrying, okay? It's only one day, Florida. What can she do in twenty-four hours?" he asks, swiping a mass of shaggy blond hair away from his eyes.

I shrug and pull my house key from under my shirt. I don't know what she can do in twenty-four hours, but I wish I didn't have to find out.

Turning to walk away, I freeze in my tracks. "Wait!"

Andrew whirls around and pulls an earbud out of his ear. "Yeah?"

"Why'd you want me to talk about what happened

in the graveyard in front of Richie? I was trying to be nice and not freak him out, you know."

He smiles. "I know. But he wants to help. And even though he's got the whole coim . . . et . . . whatever, he's really smart. Freakishly smart. He won't tell me for sure, but I'm positive he aced all his classes last year. I figure if there's anyone who might be able to make sense of something as crazy as what we saw, it could be him."

"Okay," I say hesitantly. "But if he starts having nightmares because of that or his phobia gets any worse, I'm blaming you." I jokingly punch the palm of my hand with my fist in an attempt to look intimidating.

Andrew's lips turn up into a smile as he puts the earbud back in. "I'll keep that in mind, Woodward. See ya later."

32

I OPEN THE FRONT DOOR AND WAIT FOR THE blast of cold air to hit me, but it doesn't. That's a good sign, I suppose. There's music tinkling in the kitchen and the house feels warm . . . toasty, like those radiators are really working today.

My eyes land on my mom's phone and a pang of guilt hits me. I should call Rachel. I miss her, I really, really do. But the idea of having Mom lurking around, waiting for me to return her phone while I try to quietly fill Rachel in on the ghost stuff, and Cassidy, and Andrew's freckles, is awful. I need more privacy than that.

"Tessa?" My mom's voice floats out from the kitchen and I follow it in, surprised to see she looks miserable. Bags hang under her normally bright eyes, and her face is splotchy.

Oh, no. Inez has done something to my mother. Anger, red-hot like smoldering coals, takes over me, leaving me almost breathless. I'm ready to strangle this ghost with my bare hands if I have to. Before I can stop, I pound a fist on the table, startling even myself. I didn't notice Jonah in the corner before, but he's there. It takes less than five seconds for him to start bawling.

I walk over and give him a hug. "I'm sorry buddy, I'm just mad."

He swipes at his runny nose with his sleeve. Gross. Then he reaches under the table and pulls out Reno. His mouth moves ever so slightly and I swear he's staring at me.

Turning back to Mom, I take a deep breath and try to remind myself that I'm not alone. I'm safe. I glance back at Reno's eyes, noticing that they're still fixed on me. *The doll is not after me. The doll is not after me. The doll is not after me.*

Mom puts her hands on my shoulders. "Tessa, you look kinda rough. Are you okay?"

"I don't know. What happened while I was gone?"

She looks around the room and sighs loudly. "Nothing specific. It's just that I finally got through every last box in the garage and the supplies aren't in there. I don't know where they could have gone."

"Oh! I found them!" I practically scream. "They were stacked up next to my bed earlier today." My eyes cut a path to our kitchen counter. The same counter I left the note on before I went to the library with Andrew and Nina.

It's empty.

"I left you a note over there, telling you that I found them and that they were in my room. You didn't see it?"

Mom follows the line of my finger and stares at the empty counter. "I've been here all day and I never saw a note. Was it tiny? I mean, could it have blown off and onto the floor when someone walked by?"

My stomach sinks. "It was a piece of used sketch paper."

Mom's mouth turns downward. "That's heavy paper. And too big to just vanish." She turns to look at Jonah. "Honey, did you see the paper?"

Jonah lifts Reno into a sitting position. His creepy wooden mouth opens into a silent scream and then suddenly clamps back shut, the wood-on-wood sound echoing through the kitchen and making me jump. Moving Reno closer to his ear, my little brother acts like he's listening. Like the doll is telling him something.

Suddenly, Jonah's eyes go big. "I didn't see it. But I think Reno did . . ."

Mom looks at me, then back at Jonah. She takes a few steps toward him and playfully ruffles his hair. "Well, okay, sweetie. Did he tell you if he might have touched it?"

Reno's head slowly swivels toward Mom. Jonah mumbles something under his breath and then the doll's head snaps in my direction until his beady eyes are resting on me again. I look away, unable to control the shivers building inside me.

"Reno didn't touch it, but the ghost did," Jonah says, a sinister little smile touching his lips.

I back away from Reno. Terror sweeps through me like a tidal wave, and it takes all my energy not to grab one of our kitchen knives and take it to that doll right here and now. I look to Mom for help, my palms going completely clammy.

Instead of screaming, or dousing Reno with gasoline so we can torch him, Mom just chuckles. "I see. Well, if your little buddy there sees the ghost again, could you have him give it a message for Mommy?"

A message? Is my mom crazy?

Jonah looks at me and clutches Reno to his chest. "But Tessa said there are no ghosts. Right, Tessa?"

Once upon a time, I believed ghosts didn't exist.

I was so sure of it that I told my little brother there was no such thing. But now . . . I know I was wrong. Inez exists, and she's not going to stop messing with me, my house, or my family until I figure out exactly what she wants.

If Andrew were here, I'd tell him how wrong he was. I haven't even made it one hour out of twenty-four and already I'm dying to leave.

I pass Mom the box I found in my room, happy to see her smiling again. "This is it. Just make sure everything is there." *Because an angry, unpredictable ghost moved them,* I think.

Mom pulls me into a hug. "I will, and thank you so much, honey. But I forgot to ask—how did it get into your room to begin with?"

How do I answer that? I could tell her that I believe we're being haunted and that I'm terrified, but all that would do is upset her. Ruin all her hopes of getting us settled in and happy in our new home. Or worse, she might think I'm making it up—that I want her to hate our house as much as I do. No, I won't do that to her. Especially since I'm so close to figuring out what Inez wants and how to stop her. If things get worse, I'll tell Mom and Dad. Until then, Inez is my problem to deal with.

"I don't really know; I'm just glad I found them. But can I . . . would it be okay if I made a suggestion about the way things run around here?"

Mom nods, a huge grin spreading across her face. This is right up her alley—me making suggestions for the household. Taking charge of my destiny, or so she calls it. Mom loves it when I step up and get involved, and this time, I'm going to.

"I really think I need a phone. If I'd had my own phone, the whole boxes thing wouldn't have been a problem because I would have just called or texted you. Leaving notes isn't a very reliable way to do things anymore." I stop and take a breath, my gaze landing on her face so I can gauge how she's handling my request.

"But we do still have the corkboard," she responds, setting the box in her arms down. "I just haven't gotten around to unpacking it yet. That would be a central place for us to leave messages, right?"

I roll my shoulders. "I guess, but it isn't the same. I'm making friends here now, Mom. Andrew and Nina . . . and Richie. They're nice and I want to be able to talk to them outside school, but it's hard because we've only got the one house line and I know I shouldn't tie that up."

The question I really want to ask is perched on the tip

of my tongue. Mom has always seemed so against mobile phones, but she's never told me why. I run through a list of possible reasons in my head. It is because of radiation? Monthly bills? Annoying ring tones?

"Why do you hate phones so much?"

Laughter bursts from her mouth, surprising me. "I don't hate phones!"

Tilting my head to the side, I do my best impression of Andrew when he's skeptical. "Are you sure? Because it seems like you do."

Mom shakes her head. "I don't hate phones; I hate the way they interfere with our experiences. Here's an example: say you go on an amazing vacation, like to the fjords in Norway. A lot of your friends would spend most of their time taking pictures and posting them to social media, then waiting for likes and comments. They wouldn't actually be experiencing the moment. The beauty. *Anything*."

"So you're afraid that if you give me a phone, I'll stop appreciating our vacations and trips and stuff?"

Mom rests a hand on my shoulder. "No. I'm afraid you'll forget how to appreciate them without other people telling you they're worth appreciating. Does that make sense?"

I nod, finally understanding. Mom once told me she sees a story in everything. A lopsided sand castle at high tide might look terrible but could have been built by a future architect. A small blob of jellyfish glistening in the sand might seem harmless but could be more dangerous than a vial of poison. A rainbow might be the brightest one you've ever seen but could be the result of a hurricane. Mom sees the stories, then uses them to decide what she wants to paint—it's part of what makes her such a good artist! I think she wants me to do the same . . . to experience the world, not just snap a picture of it and hope I hit a hundred likes.

"Maybe we could meet in the middle," I say, thinking out loud. "What if I get a phone so I can stay in touch with my friends but don't put any social media on it?"

Mom goes quiet. She doesn't look upset or angry, though, just thoughtful. "I'll talk to your father about it. Okay?" She gives me another quick squeeze and drops a kiss on my forehead. The smell of lavender washes over me. "But no promises."

No promises. That's better than no. I'll take it.

"Oh, I almost forgot!" Her eyes light up suddenly and she reaches into the pocket on her chunky sweater and pulls out a light pink envelope. "It's from Rachel. So nice to see you guys staying in touch like this. I don't know why people gave up writing letters to each other. They're so much more thoughtful than a phone call."

I take the envelope and run my fingers over Rachel's loopy handwriting. She's drawn little hearts around my name and smiley faces in all the *o*s. Sliding a finger under the edge, I start tearing. When Mom and Dad first told me we were moving, I was afraid Rachel would replace me. I thought it would kill me if she made a new best friend and they did all the things we were planning to do together without me. I'm beginning to realize I was wrong.

As the words inside Rachel's card come into view, I smile. I still don't want her to replace me, but I'm starting to realize that can't happen. You can't replace people. No matter how much I grow to love Andrew, Richie, and Nina, they'll never *replace* Rachel. I remember the song my mom used to sing to me when I was tiny—

MAKE NEW FRIENDS, BUT KEEP THE OLD.
ONE IS SILVER AND THE OTHER IS GOLD.
A CIRCLE IS ROUND; IT HAS NO END.
THAT'S HOW LONG I'M GOING TO BE
YOUR FRIEND.

So crazy that she used to sing me that song way before she knew I'd ever need it. But I'm glad she did. Because it all makes sense now.

33

Hi Rachel!

Wow. Congrats on getting the lead in the school play! That's awesome. And with your voice, you're going to be the best Mary Poppins they ever had. I'm sorry I didn't write you sooner BTW. Crazy stuff here still.

But the ghost thing is going better. Casper isn't really Casper at all, but a little girl named Inez. Sometime if you come visit me (please?), I'll show you everything I've learned. Trust me, though . . . it's spooky. If it weren't for Andrew, Nina, and Richie I probably would have tried to walk back to Florida by now!

Love,

Tessa

My brain has officially quit working. It's Sunday morning and even though I should be sleeping in, I've been awake and staring at the secret drawings for over two hours. I've memorized every angle, every line, every little speck of shading in them. Unfortunately, it hasn't helped. I'm still just as confused as I was before.

What if I never figure this out? The thought worries me. Inez woke me up and led me to the loose brick in the middle of the night for a reason, and I don't think it was so she could prove that the house inspector was crummy. It was because she's trying to tell me something. I hope I don't let her down.

I'm just about to give up when something dawns on me. The window in the bedroom drawing isn't square like most windows are. It's oval. Oval windows are rare, like brick walls on the inside of a house. Lucky for me, I've seen one before. Here. On Shady Street.

The spare bedroom!

Leaping off my bed, I head down the hall. The spare bedroom is where we're storing the stuff that doesn't have a place here yet. I haven't spent more than five minutes in there since we arrived, but I didn't think it mattered because there's nothing but boxes in there anyway. Maybe that's what Inez was trying to tell me; maybe there *is* something in there.

Rounding the corner into the spare room, I stop short so I don't fall over a cluster of cardboard. The room is almost completely filled with boxes. Big boxes, small boxes, long boxes, and short boxes. How do we even own this much stuff? Hurdling the first wave of them, I plant myself directly in front of the oval window and then lift the drawing into the air for comparison. Jackpot! It's identical. I'm in the right place. I have to be!

Sitting down with my legs crossed, I spread out the second drawing on the floor. Yup. Still looks like a music box. I briefly wonder if there could be a music box somewhere in this room, then tell myself I'm being crazy. The only stuff in here is our stuff, and we don't own a music box.

Unless . . .

My gaze flits to the small door on the other side of the room. It's the same door I grilled Dad about when we first moved in, the one that's so small and warped it looks like a troll could hobble out of it at any moment.

"What is that?" I asked, lowering a bag of bedsheets to the floor.

"It's for storage. A lot of older houses have them."

"Storage?" I snorted. "It's so small! What, was it made for elves or something?"

Dad laughed and said the door was deceptive. That there was probably much more space behind it than it seemed. Then he reminded me of how old this house is and promised that once everything was unpacked, we'd pry open the door and see if there were any treasures inside. I wasn't expecting to find anything in there before, but now I'm not so sure.

Taking a deep breath to steady my nerves, I walk over to it. The door is so short that the top barely comes up to my waist. Bending down, I grip the knob and give it a tug. It doesn't budge. No wonder Dad said we'd have to pry it open. It's sealed shut.

My brain swims with questions. Was the door sealed on purpose or did people just accidentally paint over it year after year? And how long has it been since someone opened it and looked inside? Too long, I decide. For all I know, it's filled with spiders and spider eggs and all kinds of disgusting spider stuff.

I hate spiders.

"All right, all right. Spiders or no spiders, I'm coming in," I mutter, kneeling down. Using the scissors Mom cuts packing tape with, I carefully start chipping away at the seal, smiling at the paint chips that begin raining down to the floor. It's working! When it finally looks like most of the seal is broken, I grab the knob and pull as hard as I can. This time a sharp crack echoes out over the room and the door flies open. I tumble backward, landing on my butt and completely flattening a box that says MEMORIES on the top. Oops. Hopefully Mom took a "mental picture," as she calls it, because whatever was in this box is a goner.

Crawling off the mound of broken cardboard, I immediately bring my arm up over my nose. An old, musty smell has wafted into the room. It reminds me of my grandma's basement.

I drop down onto my hands and knees and peer into the black space. Even without much light, I can tell there's something in there. Something big. Fear grips me. Suddenly the idea of spiders doesn't seem so bad. Holding my breath, I shove my hand into the opening and start feeling around. An icy draft rips through the room, making my teeth chatter.

She's watching me.

"Is this right?" I ask in a shaky voice. I'm so scared that it's hard to make words come out. "Am I close? *Please.* Tell me I'm close!"

My hand finds something hard in the darkness. I drag the item out into the light. It's a wooden box. A crate, actually. The top is covered with a blanket, and there's black writing on the side that says

BASEMENT FINDS. Basement? There isn't a basement in this house; underneath the first floor is a garage.

Ahhhh. Right. It wasn't always a garage. Dad told me that the basement was dug out several years ago to make the garage. This box must have been stuff the owners found when they cleaned it out!

Gently, I begin removing the blanket that stretches across the top of the crate. A cloud of dust billows into my face. Well, that answers one question. It's been a *very* long time since someone opened that door.

My breath catches as I stare at the crate's contents. There's a weathered-looking metal toy on the top. It's rusted out in several places and has one of those windup thingies sticking out of its side. Packed just under the toy are a stack of old postcards, a pair of tin cups, a brass doorknob, and . . .

Every muscle in my body stiffens. The last object in the crate is a box. *A music box.*

34

"NO WAY!" NINA BREATHES OUT, ROTATING THE music box in her hands so she can examine it from every angle. I used my mom's phone to call her as soon as I pulled it from the crate, and then she called Andrew. Thanks to their trusty Schwinns, I was sneaking them in our back door less than ten minutes later. Guess they must've talked their way out of family day after all. "This is incredible. And definitely old. Where was it again?"

Guilt gnaws at me. Even though I think I did the right thing by following Inez's clues alone, I feel bad about it. I feel even worse that I wasn't brave enough to open the music box alone.

"In the spare room storage closet." I watch Nina

carefully hand the music box to Andrew. This is it. I have to show them the drawings. I reach behind the crate and grab the roll. The twine dangles from it limply. "I'm guessing that when the basement was cleared out to be made into a garage, the owners didn't even really look at this stuff. They just tossed it into a crate and dumped it in there."

"Amazing," Nina says, shaking her head. "I can't believe you found it!"

"Yeah. Well, there . . . uh . . . there were some hints that I might find it there."

"Hints?" Andrew asks. "What kind of hints?"

The truth spills out so fast I barely think about what I'm saying. "I was sleeping and there was this sound and then the loose brick and the drawings and one was of an oval window and—"

"Whooooa," Nina says, cutting off my rant. "Sounds? Loose brick? Oval window? You aren't making any sense."

Andrew sets the music box down on the floor between us. He stares at me pointedly. "The ghost showed you how to find this?"

I nod.

"When?" he presses. His tone isn't angry or accusing. It's worried.

"Four days ago, on Wednesday."

Nina gasps. "*Four* days ago? Why didn't you tell us about it?"

"I think she wanted me to follow the clues alone. She led me to this." I point at the box, nervous all over again about what's inside.

"So you followed the hints and found this box. Then what?" Andrew prompts.

"I got scared."

It feels even worse to admit it than I thought it would. Truth is, I've been scared a lot since the haunting started. Scared of the sounds at night, scared of the changing painting, scared of Reno. But the thing I think I'm most scared of is looking like a coward in front of my new friends. Nina is . . . well, Nina. She's smart and kind and brave. And Andrew is more than just a soccer player with cute freckles. He's the best friend I have here.

"I'm sorry," I say, running a finger along the delicate flowers carved into the corners of the music box. A single tear paves its way down my cheek. I brush it away, embarrassed. "I wanted to surprise you guys by solving this whole thing, but I couldn't. I need help."

Andrew scoots over closer, smashing me into Nina. He slings an arm around both of us. "Is it mean to say I'm glad? I mean, we've come this far—*together.* It would've kinda sucked if you'd figured it out without us, Florida."

"I second that," Nina adds. Her normally tousled hair is braided tightly down her back today, and her research journal is resting in her lap. Her eyes land on the drawings in my hand. "Are those the clues that led you to the closet?"

"Oh. Yeah." Unrolling them, I spread them out. "This is a drawing of the spare bedroom. It looks different and all because there's boxes there right now instead of furniture, but I recognized it from the window. And this—" I tap on the second drawing. "This is of the music box. See the flowers?"

Nina holds the drawing up to the music box. "I'm impressed."

"With the drawings?" I ask.

She laughs, rolling her fishbowl eyes like I'm nuts. "No, Tess. With *you!* These weren't easy clues to figure out."

"I agree. This is crazy," Andrew adds, examining the drawings. "Where did you say they were hidden?"

"Behind a loose brick in the wall in our living room." I remember the sound that woke me up that night—the concrete clink of the brick sliding back into place—and shiver. "She woke me up to look back there. I'm sure of it."

"Wow." Andrew rubs the back of his neck. He looks awed. "Not gonna lie, Surfer Girl, I would have probably chickened out!"

Warmth creeps over my cheeks. I *did* almost chicken out. A bunch of times! I'm so glad I didn't. I'm also glad I waited to open the music box with them. Even though it was embarrassing to admit that I was scared, this feels right. Good.

"So the mystery is solved." Andrew brushes his hands together like he's getting dust off them. "Inez *was* an artist. That's why she's haunting you."

"Meh, not so fast, Sherlock. We still haven't figured out how the statue vanished, why there was no Inez Clarke in the census, or what she wants. Plus, there's this." I flip the drawings over to reveal the letters on the back. *"I. B."*

A rush of air escapes Nina's lips. Her face is pale, her eyes impossibly wide. "Ohhhhhh, no."

"What? *Oh, no,* what? What does *I. B.* mean?" Andrew looks from the drawings to me, then back again.

"Don't you see?" Nina asks him. "This only complicates things more! Yeah, the pictures tie the ghost to this house. I mean, she couldn't have drawn the spare bedroom unless she'd seen it before, right? But the initials on the back don't match up. We've been focused on Inez *Clarke* all this time, and these letters *might* mean that whoever drew the pictures had a last name that begins with *B*."

"Maybe they aren't initials," Andrew offers. "Could they mean something else? International bananas. Interstellar bacon. Impressive bologna."

"Interstellar bacon?" I deadpan, fighting the urge to laugh. "Are you crazy, Andrew?"

He clutches his gurgling stomach. "No. Just hungry."

I form a circle with my hands and reach out as if I'm going to strangle him, but Nina stops me. Lifting the music box off the floor, she holds it out for me to take. "Open."

"Me? Why me?" I ask.

"Oh, gee, I don't know. Maybe because it's your ghost?" she teases. "C'mon, Tess. If the ghost really led you to this music box, we need to know what's in it."

She's right. I can't go on like this forever—looking over my shoulder, sleeping on the couch, digging around in the walls. It's time to end this.

I crack the lid of the music box. A soft, metallic tinkling sound echoes out. Music. "Oh my gosh . . . it works."

Andrew and Nina huddle closer. This is what I wanted, what I needed. Even though I'm the one opening the box, they're here with me. Supporting me. If Inez herself were to spring out right now, I think we could handle it.

A tiny metal ring lies in the bottom of the music box, along with another paper. It's folded up, so I doubt it's a drawing. I slide the ring onto my pinky finger, then unfold the paper. It's a death certificate.

For Inez.

35

MY MIND IS A JUMBLE OF CONFUSED THOUGHTS. A death certificate for Inez. That's what it looks like, but is it possible?

Andrew's hand trembles as he reaches for the paper. I squint to make sure I'm seeing the words correctly. "*Inez Briggs?* What? How?"

"I'm not sure yet, but this can't be a coincidence. It's a death certificate for a little girl named Inez Briggs who died on August 1, 1880. That's the same day that Inez Clarke died. In Chicago, too! It's got to be the same girl, right?"

"And that last name . . . Briggs. As in Amos Briggs," I sputter out.

Nina's mouth is hanging open and I can see every

centimeter of her perfectly straight teeth. "Let me see that."

We stay silent for a few moments while she examines the certificate. It's grainy and yellowed, but the writing is clear as day. *Inez Briggs. Graceland Cemetery.*

"Diphtheria. This says she died of diphtheria. I don't know much about it, but I know a lot of people who lived back when Inez was alive contracted it. It was some kind of bacterial infection . . . something that affected the throat." Nina looks at Andrew and me. "If this certificate is for the same girl, wouldn't the cause of death say 'lightning strike'?" she asks.

Andrew scoots over so he can rest his back against the wall. "No, not if that isn't true. Maybe that's just part of the legend. Maybe there's more to Inez Clarke—I mean, Inez Briggs—than people know."

"You mean like maybe she lived in my house?" The second I ask it, I realize how scary my question really is. It's obvious that my house is haunted, but I never considered that it could be haunted because the person who died used to *live* here. Did she sleep in my room? Eat in our kitchen? Use our bathrooms?

Eww. Never mind.

I freeze as another thought pops into my head. A darker one. Maybe the ghost didn't just live in my house; maybe she *died* here, too. I drag my hands down my face, nauseated at the idea. "Mom and Dad got a deal on this house. They said so themselves."

"I like cherry pie," Andrew volunteers.

"What?" Nina asks. "What does cherry pie have to do with anything?"

"Oh, sorry. Tessa just said something totally random, so I thought that's what we were doing." Andrew ducks as I lob a ball of wadded-up packing tape in his direction.

"It's not random, Andrew! It's true. They bragged about what a steal this house is. Do you think—" I pause, horrified by what I'm about to say. "Do you think it's because Inez died here? In this house?"

"Ack!" Andrew jumps to his feet and looks around. "Gross, Tess!"

"I'm not trying to be gross! I'm being serious. It's possible!"

Nina runs a finger over the faded letters on the paper. "Relax, guys. According to this, she didn't even live here, so she probably didn't die here, either. This lists Inez Briggs's address as on Center Street. You live on *Shady* Street."

"She's right," Andrew says. "I've never heard of Center Street. It probably isn't even in this neighborhood."

The drawings from behind the brick pop into

my head. "If that's true, how would she have known about the oval window in the spare bedroom?"

Crickets.

"*And* what about the *I. B.* on the back of them? That totally makes sense if her name was Inez Briggs."

More crickets. Awesome. They're just as confused as me.

"*And* if she didn't live here, why is my house haunted to begin with? Why the heck would the painting keep changing and the face show up in the mirror and stupid Reno start crying?"

"Reno?" Andrew and Nina ask simultaneously. They look at each other and shrug.

"Remember? The demonic doll I told you about?"

Andrew's face changes suddenly. Instead of looking confused and tired, he looks excited. "Wait! You said it isn't a normal doll, right?"

"Yeah, it's a ventriloquist dummy. My dad bought it at a yard sale." I shiver, thinking about Reno's creepy black eyes and cold wooden face.

Andrew snaps his head back toward Nina. "Google that. Google ventriloquist dummies and see if you can come up with how long they've been around."

"Why?" I ask, but he waves me off.

"Bingo!" Nina whisper-yells, tilting her phone toward us. I lean to look over her shoulder.

It's a collection of ventriloquist dummies over the years. I don't see one that looks exactly like Reno, but several of them are close. "Ventriloquist dummies have been around for hundreds of years. Some of these were from the eighteen hundreds—back when vaudeville was just getting big."

"Back when Inez was alive," I whisper.

"Exactly. Maybe she chose to use the doll to try to communicate with you because it was familiar to her! Think of all the technology and stuff they didn't have back when she was alive—I bet any one of our houses would be confusing to a two-hundred-plus-year-old ghost!" Nina says.

"This is crazy!" Andrew says. There's a spark in his eyes now. It's bright, and even though we're discussing ghosts, I feel better. Happy.

"Do you think that could be the explanation, Tessa?" Nina asks. Her tone is hopeful.

I nod and hand her phone back to her. "According to this site, vaudeville-style entertainment started getting big in the early eighteen eighties—right before Inez was born. I originally thought she was using Reno to scare me because I hate him, but maybe it's because she was excited to see something familiar."

A pang of sadness hits me. Sadness for Inez. If

the death certificate *is* hers, that means her grave site is wrong. Every story about her is wrong. She wasn't just an advertisement for a local sculptor—she was a *real girl.* Her last name wasn't Clarke. And she doesn't escape her glass box during storms because she died after being hit by lightning. Her death had nothing to do with lightning!

I run my fingers over the wrinkled edges of the death certificate. As crazy as it sounds, I'm beginning to feel less afraid of Inez. I mean, if she wanted to hurt me, she would have done it by now, right?

Andrew rakes a hand through the front of his hair. He leaves it standing on end. "I'm still confused."

"That makes two of us," I mumble. "If Inez never lived in this house, then we're back to my first theory on why she chose me to haunt."

"Which was . . ." Nina prompts.

"Because she liked art. I guess it's still possible, especially since I found those drawings hidden in the wall."

Andrew folds the death certificate up and hands it to Nina. She tucks it deep in her research notebook. "But why would her death certificate have been in this basement at all if she never lived here?"

Nina taps her chin with a pen. "We don't know that the certificate is real. Not yet."

"It looks real." I wrinkle up my nose. The stink of musty paper still fills the room. "Smells real, too."

Andrew peeks through the small storage closet's door, then presses it tightly closed with the toe of his shoe. Nina blinks at it, then sighs. "I gotta go."

"What?" I jump in front of the door. "No. Don't go yet. You guys just got here and now I'm creeped out!"

"I'm sorry, Tess but we'll never figure this out if I don't do some more research. There are too many things that don't make sense." Nina grimaces and holds her notebook up.

I stare at it, amused by the fact that it's silver and glittery. Shouldn't it have a skull and crossbones on it or something? I mean, it looks more like a Christmas ornament than a notebook for ghost research.

A hand on my shoulder startles me. I look up into Andrew's worried eyes. "You going to be okay?"

"Yeah."

"Sure?"

I shrug. Even though I'd rather have them stay, I'm actually not that scared about being here alone with Inez. "I can't be positive, because, you know . . . ghosts. But I think so."

He smiles and makes his way to the door. "Good, because I'm not supposed to be out on my bike alone.

I have to leave when Nina does or my mom will freak if she finds out."

I laugh. "So you're not free-range, then, huh?"

Andrew tips his head back and lets out a loud hoot. "No. I'm half free-range and half 'you're grounded.' Remember?"

I *do* remember. Andrew told me that back when he was just a blond-haired boy in a park, covered in dirt. Back when the only help I had in surviving my new neighborhood was a beaten-up old compass, and when I believed the only nice thing in this entire city was North Pond. I chuckle at the thought of how a ratty soccer ball landing at my feet changed everything.

I was so wrong, and for once, I couldn't be happier.

36

THIS PILLOW IS ROCK-HARD, I THINK, ROLLING OVER. The temple on the right side of my head is sore and I can't seem to get comfortable. A sound startles me, something like a cross between a car backfiring and a bottle rocket. I snap upright and pry my tired eyes open.

"Well, so glad you decided to join us, Miss Woodward." Mrs. Medina is glaring at me. There's a book on the floor at her feet, probably the item that interrupted my slumber.

"Sorry," I squeak out. My mouth is dry and there's a small puddle of drool on my desk. I quickly toss a notepad over it and tell myself I'll deal with that later.

Andrew is looking at me like I've lost my mind. I do my best to straighten my back and stay awake for the rest of class. It's going to be hard; I barely slept last night. Again.

Three distinct times, I heard knocking on my door. The first time I was half asleep and thought it was Jonah, so I got up and checked. Hallway empty. Lights out. No one to be seen.

The second time, I knew it was Inez. I could tell from the way my skin got all prickly and the hairs on the back of my neck did their thing. There wasn't any crying or door rattling, but she was there. *I could feel her.*

The worst part about the whole thing wasn't being afraid; it was being confused. In the beginning, I was convinced Inez wanted to terrify me . . . or worse, hurt me. But with each day that passes, I feel less afraid and more worried. Like the ghost I've been afraid of for so long is trying to tell me something I don't understand. Is Inez trapped in my house, scared and lonely? Desperate? I crawled back into bed having no idea and feeling more helpless than ever.

"And those are factorials!" my teacher exclaims loudly, and sets her dry-erase marker back on the desk. "Any questions?"

Um, yeah. I have a ton. Why was Inez Clarke's

death certificate labeled *Inez Briggs*? Or is that some bizarre coincidence? It's still bothering me, and I haven't had a chance to research any more since Nina and Andrew left my house. I realize after the first few hands shoot up that my teacher was talking about math questions. Nope. Don't have any of those.

"All right, then. Class dismissed. Have a wonderful night, everyone."

Andrew is up and out of his chair before anyone else. He crosses to my desk and hovers over me. "Florida, you almost got yourself tossed out of here."

"No, I didn't," I yawn out. "She didn't say anything about that."

His face grows serious. "Yeah, well, be careful. Sleeping through class doesn't usually earn you a star student award, if you know what I mean."

I rub my hands over my face. I can't believe I fell asleep right in the middle of class like that. It's embarrassing! It's also not me. "I know. I'm just so tired."

"We're supposed to meet Nina and Cass on the front steps. Want me to go tell them you need to go home and take a nap instead?"

"In my house of horrors?" I chuckle grimly. "No thanks. I can stay awake, swear."

I'm already walking away when my brain finally

kicks in. I skid to a stop. "Whoa, whoa, whoa. Did you just say we're meeting Nina and *Cass*?"

Andrew frowns. "Ahhh, I thought I could slide that past you."

"It didn't work."

"Okay. Okay. I'm sorry." He eyes me for a second, then sighs loudly. "I know what you're thinking."

"Trust me, you don't," I mumble. I haven't slept well since I got to Chicago, my ghost mystery is still unsolved, and now this. "If you knew what I'm thinking, you would have ducked by now."

"Wow. Harsh. You really do need more sleep," he says with a laugh. "Look, Cass is the one who asked to hang out today. It wasn't me or Nina or Richie begging her this time. I think that's a good sign. Maybe it means whatever was bothering her is gone."

That can't be true, because I'm still here, I think. My insides wilt at the thought of spending time with Cassidy. Even digging more bricks out of my disturbing old wall back home sounds more fun.

"Just give it a chance. Please?"

I can't believe I'm agreeing to it, but I do. Andrew has done a lot for me since I moved here and I owe him this. If Cassidy is a jerk again, I'm done trying. For good.

When we step outside, Nina is already sitting on

the base of the steps. Large blue headphones cover her ears, and her nose is tucked into an e-reader of some kind. Cassidy and Richie are a few feet away, talking.

I stare at the two of them, trying to decide what's different today. I don't think it's Richie's hair. That looks just as shaggy as the day I met him. My eyes travel to Cassidy. Even though her dark locks are partly hidden by a hood, I can still see their cropped edges and the blue streak. I've just started studying their clothes when I figure it out: Cassidy is smiling.

Richie looks up and notices me. His lips curve up into an instant grin. "Hey! Woodward! Congrats!"

"Um . . . thanks?" Unless he's congratulating me on being even more confused than I was a minute ago, I'm lost. "On what, though?"

He lifts his phone to reveal a calendar app. "On surviving your first week here!"

Oh my gosh. He's right! I started school here in Chicago exactly a week ago. Since then I've made new friends, inherited a ghost, lost my compass, found a music box, and decided deep-dish pizza is ah-mazing.

"We should totally celebrate," Richie crows. "Cupcakes or ice cream?"

I sneak a glance at Andrew. He lifts his shoulders in a *whatever you want* gesture. I sigh. "I can't go. Thanks, though. I have to figure out this—" I stop talking, remembering Cassidy is there. I can't discuss the ghost in front of her. "This *thing* before I can go pig out."

"The thing," Richie repeats, his forehead wrinkling up.

"She means the ghost stuff." Cassidy jams her hands down into her jeans pockets and studies me. "And seriously, Richie, are you *always* thinking about food?"

Andrew hoots. "As if you don't know the answer to that already, Cass."

"He stopped in the cafeteria on the way here, you know. Claimed he needs to keep his blood sugar up," she adds.

"Don't judge!" Richie playfully elbows Cassidy. She laughs.

I open my mouth to chime in, but nothing comes out. Something weird is happening. Cassidy is here, talking and laughing like things are normal. She hasn't rolled her eyes, or stalked off, or given me even one *you're a mosquito* look. I could not be more surprised if I found a unicorn in my locker. I look to Andrew for an explanation, but he just shrugs.

"Richie filled me in a little," Cassidy explains. "I hope that's okay."

"Filled you in on the stuff going on in my house?"

I ask nervously. I'm not mad at Richie, exactly. He and Cassidy are obviously pretty tight. But something about her knowing this stuff makes me uncomfortable. Maybe it's because I still don't trust her.

"Yeah," she answers, fidgeting with her backpack straps. "But mostly about the glass box."

For a split second, my mind is blank. Glass box? Then I remember what she's talking about. Inez's grave!

"Richie explained what happened. It sounds like there was a thunderstorm that brought cold air in off the lake—like a cold front or something."

I nod. I remember how quickly the temperature dropped, my skin breaking out in goose bumps all over again. "Yeah, it got super-cold all of a sudden."

"I could see my breath when we left," Andrew adds with a shudder. "It was freaky."

"It wasn't a ghost," Richie states.

"Really?" Suddenly I'm *very* interested in what Cassidy has to say. "Because it felt like a ghost. And the grounds keepers at the cemetery have reported the same thing happening to them for years. The statue disappearing, I mean."

Cassidy nods. Her eyes are twinkling with excitement. "I'm sure it has happened for years, but it's not a ghost. It's science."

37

SCIENCE. I CONSIDER THIS, REMEMBERING THAT Andrew told me Cassidy and Richie are in a science club together. Could she be right? Could the explanation for the vanishing statue be scientific?

Cassidy pulls a folder from her backpack and opens it up. Then she hands me a sheet of paper. Condensation. The entire paper is about the process of condensation.

"I printed that out this morning just in case you didn't believe me. A glass box like the one Richie described would be filled with air, since it isn't vacuum-sealed. If the air inside the box was warm, but then the temperature dropped and colder air met the outside of the glass, you could end up with a bunch of condensation."

"And what looked like a missing statue," Richie adds.

My jaw drops. I learned about condensation in like, third grade or something. How did it not occur to me . . . or Nina . . . or Andrew that the explanation was something so simple?

Remembering exactly how the glass box looked, I start to feel silly. Now that I really think about it, the box didn't really look empty at all. It looked white.

"I guess that's possible," I mumble, feeling a little embarrassed. I was so afraid in that graveyard when the lightning and thunder started that I honestly believed the statue of Inez had somehow crawled out of that box and was chasing Andrew and me.

Cassidy's blue eyes sparkle. "I can't say for sure that's what happened since I wasn't there, but it's a pretty good theory. The same thing that happens to house windows sometimes, and even on shower doors. It might have looked empty inside, but my guess is that the color of the statue matched the condensation so it was sorta camouflaged."

"But if the statue had been bright red . . ." Richie prompts.

"They would have probably been able to see it!" Cassidy finishes. The two of them high-five each other, grinning like maniacs.

I think back to the look Richie gave Cassidy in the cafeteria that day. It was familiar—like they knew each other well enough to communicate silently. Now it makes sense. Science nerds. Just like Andrew said.

"Thanks for this," I say to Cassidy, jiggling the paper on condensation in the air.

A flicker of pride crosses her face. "Yeah, no problem. Hey—um, can I talk to you for a minute? Alone?"

Ten minutes ago, I would have answered no to this question without even thinking about it. But this Cassidy seems friendlier. Less angry. And she did just solve the vanishing statue thing. Maybe I should hear her out.

"Sure. Can you watch my stuff?" I ask Andrew. Worry twists his expression. I feel bad for him. I know how important it is to him that Cassidy and I get along. It's important to me, too. But I can't be the only one who's trying to make this work. I look down at the paper on condensation, hopeful. Maybe I'm not anymore . . .

I follow Cassidy over to the edge of the school building. Just far enough away that no one can hear us if we talk in normal voices, but close enough that if I scream, they'll hear me. Better safe than sorry.

Cassidy takes a deep breath. "I wanted to apologize. For the way I acted before, I mean."

"Oh. That. Thanks. I wasn't sure what to think. I mean, other than that you obviously hated me."

Cassidy shakes her head. "It wasn't you. Not really, anyway. I've had some bad stuff going on at home and when you showed up . . ." She trails off, lost in a memory. "I don't know. I guess you could say it was bad timing."

"Bad timing for you?" I laugh. "I'm the one who had to move to a new school a month into seventh grade."

Cassidy snorts. "Yeah, that sucks. I moved here in first grade and even then it wasn't fun." She glances over at Richie and Andrew. They're taking turns throwing pretzels at each other's open mouths. "These guys are my best friends. My only friends, really."

"And you were afraid I was taking them away from you?" I ask.

"Maybe. Ugh. I don't know." She leans against the building, her hood slipping off her head. I can't help but notice that when she isn't frowning, Cassidy is really pretty. "I've never been very good with asking for help, or whatever. But I'm trying to get better."

Interesting. Andrew said Cassidy likes her privacy, but maybe it's more than that. I think back on how embarrassed I was to tell Andrew and Nina that I couldn't open the music box by myself. Even though I knew they wouldn't laugh, admitting my fear made me feel silly. Weak. Is that how Cassidy felt? Like sharing her problems would make her look like a coward? Too bad she can't see herself the way her friends do. Andrew described Cassidy as creative and thoughtful. Nina said she has a crazy hyena laugh. And although I don't know her that well, I think I would describe her as . . . bold. When she's not glaring at me, that is.

"Anyway, I was planning on telling them about my parents and how much they've been fighting." She stops talking suddenly, as if she said something she shouldn't have. An awkward silence settles between us.

"I thought a cement statue was chasing me," I offer sheepishly. "If that isn't something to be embarrassed of, then fighting parents definitely isn't."

Relief smooths out the worried lines in her face. "Thanks. I guess I chickened out of talking to them."

"Because of me," I say. It seems so obvious now. Cassidy is having a rough time at home. She was working up the courage to tell her best friends about it, but by the time she did, they were busy helping me. I know Andrew and Nina didn't mean to hurt her feelings, but I get it. "I wasn't just trying to get attention. And I wasn't making the ghost stuff up, either. I wouldn't do that. Swear."

"Oh, I know. I mean, I thought you were making it up at first, but then Richie said he saw you guys coming out of the library and then I knew you must really believe it." She smirks. "I think that *might* have been Andrew's first time in a library."

Mmm-hmm. No wonder Andrew didn't know where anything was in there! He tried to say it was because they rearranged, but Nina's *whatever* look gave him away. "Did you tell Richie? About the problems—er, stuff—at home?"

Cass nods. "Yeah. I think all the ghost talk wigged him out, so he hung out with me a lot this week. That's how I knew about the glass case at the cemetery."

I can't help it. I laugh. "I don't think ghost hunting is in his future."

"I don't think anything that isn't molecules, soccer balls, or hot dogs is." Cassidy giggles. Richie yells in the background—something about Andrew being a big fat cheat at the pretzel-throwing game. We laugh harder.

"Thanks again. For helping with the research and all."

Cassidy's mouth lifts into a half-smile. "No prob. It was actually nice to have something else to focus on besides my problems. Fun, even." She laughs weakly. "Maybe I should be thanking you."

"I'll keep you in mind if anything else disappears. Ahhh, I should probably go," I say, hiking a thumb in Andrew's direction. "We still have some things to figure out. Did . . . did you want to stay?"

She considers it for a second, then shakes her head. "Nah, I'm good. Another time, though."

Nodding, I give a small wave as she walks back toward Andrew and Nina to say goodbye. The unease in the pit of my stomach slowly begins to fade. Things might not be perfect, but they're better. Cassidy said there will be another time—a time when she does stay and hang out with all of us—and this time I believe her.

38

"EVERYTHING OKAY?" ANDREW ASKS. HE'S leaning against the railing of the school steps and the sun is landing on his hair, making it look lighter than it actually is. "You're not bleeding or swearing, so I assume so."

I laugh and nod. "Yeah, we're cool."

"Good." He beams. "I was hoping you'd say that."

"So, what is she doing? She's been staring at that screen since we got out here." I point to Nina.

"Um, not sure. But I think she's in her happy place."

I creep up behind Nina and look over her shoulder. There's a video rolling on her screen. I can't tell exactly what it is, but I do see gravestones. In fact, I see Inez's gravestone. "Yup. It's her happy place."

I giggle and tap her on the shoulder.

"Ahh!" Nina screams and jumps to her feet. Her e-reader tumbles from her lap and lands on the cement with a nauseating crack. The jack to her headphones dangles in front of her and her expression changes from surprise to worry.

"Oh my god. Nina, I'm so sorry!" I rush forward and grab the e-reader, flipping it over and exhaling the breath I've been holding. It isn't broken. Not even one crack. "It's fine. Just a little dinged up on the side."

Nina takes it from my hand and turns it over in hers. Then she smiles the biggest smile I've ever seen on her. "Even if it had been broken, it would have been okay."

"Because you secretly hate e-readers and that one got what it deserved?" Andrew asks, an annoying smirk playing on his face.

"No, smarty-pants. Because I think I just solved our mystery once and for all," Nina says. A jolt of excitement runs through me. Could she really have solved it?

I wave my hands in the air impatiently. "C'mon! Don't keep us waiting!"

Nina tilts the screen toward us.

"What are we looking at?" Andrew asks.

"A documentary on Chicago ghosts with a focus

on Inez Clarke . . . er, Briggs. I've watched it from beginning to end twice, then also done some research on the side to see if there's any truth to it."

"And?" I ask impatiently. I can't help it. I have to know what she knows. Now!

"And it turns out that you are holding the missing link!" she nearly screams.

"The missing link? What are you talking about?"

"The death certificate we found. It's real, Tessa. It has to be."

I let her words sink in, my mind wandering back to the moment I pulled that slip of paper out of the music box. Andrew and Nina's faces were white. Sheet white. The boxes were so dust-covered it looked like no one had touched them in years. The door was sealed shut . . . painted over and forgotten.

Is Nina right? Could that certificate *actually* be real? I run a finger over the small metal ring on my pinky and breathe deeply.

Andrew lowers himself down to the pavement with us. "Whoa, I'm officially lost. Start at the beginning, Ghost Girl."

Nina cracks a grin at the nickname. "Okay. After the documentary, I started my research with Mary Clarke. I found out that her first marriage was to a man with the last name of Briggs!"

"Briggs! Like Amos? Did they have a son?" Andrew asks.

"No. No. Remember, Amos Briggs isn't in the Chicago census, either. Actually, Inez was Mary's daughter from her first marriage!"

I suck in a giant lungful of air. Inez Briggs. "Wait, so are you saying Inez Clarke was definitely, for one hundred percent sure, actually Inez Briggs?"

Nina nods. "Yup! It looks like maybe the name was a simple transcription error. They used her mother's new married name on the gravestone instead of her proper last name of Briggs!"

So we were right. Inez *didn't* die from a lightning strike. It was diphtheria. Was that why she kept messing with the electricity in my house and blowing huge storms up around me? Was it a message? I think about the way the electricity crackled and burned under my skin, like a lit sparkler on the Fourth of July. Maybe that was Inez's way of telling me that the lightning strike stories are all wrong.

Andrew looks thoughtful. "So the Amos Briggs name on the cemetery plot records was also just a mistake?"

Nina nods again. "Yup. When spoken, *Amos Briggs* sounds a little like *Inez Briggs,* and so the wrong name was recorded."

"One girl. Two huge mistakes." I say, shaking my head. I feel so bad for her. "What else?"

Nina unloops her headphones from her neck and meets my eyes. "I also found proof that when Inez died from diphtheria, she was living with her grandparents on Center Street."

Center Street. I remember that address from the death certificate. My skin tingles with anticipation. I stand up so I can pace back and forth.

"Shortly after Inez died, her mother, Mary Clarke, was questioned—probably something to do with life insurance, according to all these websites—and she claimed she didn't have a daughter," Nina finishes.

My mind is boggled. Why would Inez's mother have denied her? Was Inez sent to live with her grandparents because she was sick? Or was it because her mother didn't want her anymore? My heart aches for this girl.

"Center Street," Andrew murmurs, sliding his finger across his cell phone screen. "Huh. This says their home was in the neighborhood we call Uptown now."

I have no idea where Uptown is, so I just look to Nina for confirmation. She nods and shows me the neighborhood on a map. "Uptown isn't far from here. I don't know where her original residence was, but according to a few of these websites and a couple of pretty knowledgeable historians, it could have been in Lincoln Park."

A hush falls over our group. Andrew finally speaks. "You were right, Tess."

Goose bumps break out on my arms and legs. The loose brick and the *I. B.* on the back of the drawings spring to mind. Inez was trying to tell me who she was all along. "My house was Inez's original residence."

Nina lifts her chin in a quick nod. "Seems so. I think that's why no one has solved this mystery yet. Without a death certificate, all these theories about Inez's statue were just that . . . *theories.* When that box of Inez's old stuff got locked away and forgotten, so did the truth."

The truth. Inez led me to it after all. The loose brick. The wooden crate. The music box . . . they were her clues. Her bread crumbs.

"If Inez really did live in your house, maybe her ghost still haunts it because she was forced to move," Andrew suggests.

I sink back down onto the cracked pavement, a familiar feeling of sadness sweeping over me. I was forced to leave Fort Myers and it felt terrible. But at least I have my parents with me, and Jonah. How would I feel if I had to move without them? Like Inez? Terrible, I think.

I roll the idea around in my head, feeling strangely calm. All this time I thought Inez reached out to me because she was a budding artist, and maybe she was, but the possibility that my new house on Shady Street is the real connection makes so much sense. The rattling doorknobs and wailing. The possessed bathroom and the painting in the stairwell. The death certificate, tucked away in a musty old music box. It all makes sense now.

Pride swells in me. I might have been terrified, and I might have failed at more than a few things along the way, but I still did something special. I solved the mystery.

Inez Clarke used to live in my house. No, Inez *Briggs* used to live in my house.

39

BACK IN FLORIDA, WE HAD A LOT OF STORMS in the summer. They'd sweep in during the late afternoon, blacken the sky and scatter the gulls. But they weren't cold like they are here in Chicago. They were warm, and afterward the beach always seemed so clean. So peaceful, like even though the storms were freaky at the time, they happened for a reason.

Sounds nuts, but that's how I feel right now. Like everything with Inez has happened for a reason. The thought sends a blanket of calm over me.

"Tessa?" There's a long pause, followed by a sigh. "I think she's in shock."

I blink off the haze, suddenly realizing that Andrew and Nina are both staring at me. "What?"

"You've been quiet for a really long time," Nina says. Her hands are clasped in a worried knot. "Are you okay?"

Looking from her to Andrew and back again, I chuckle. "Yeah. Actually, I am."

"I'm impressed, Florida. If I found out the kind of stuff you just did, I'd probably be putting a for-sale sign in my front yard." Andrew takes one last look at the image of the cemetery on Nina's e-reader, then hands it back to her. "You're really okay with all this?"

Standing, I look out over the school lawn. The sign by the parking lot still says WELCOME BACK TO SCHOOL. The first time I saw that sign, I was sitting in the car with my dad and wanted nothing more than to leave. Now? I like it. I have friends here—good friends—and Chicago isn't half bad. Sure, it still smells a little like a toilet sometimes, but Mom was right—there's beauty if you take the time to look for it. Plus, there's a Starbucks on pretty much every corner, and who doesn't love vanilla bean Frappuccinos?

I can't help but think that maybe Inez understood me somehow. After all, she had to move, like me, and when she got sick with diphtheria, she didn't even have her parents at her side. It must have been lonely.

Maybe even more lonely than I was after moving here from Florida.

"I really am okay. This whole thing has been scary, but there's definitely a silver lining."

Andrew looks perplexed. "Silver lining to being haunted?"

Nodding, I waggle a finger at them.

"Us?" Nina asks, laughing. "How are we a silver lining?"

"Think about it," I say. "When I came here, I didn't know anyone. If Inez hadn't scared me with the flickering lights in my bathroom, I wouldn't have gone to North Pond."

Andrew's face brightens. "And if you hadn't gone to North Pond, we wouldn't have met!"

I look down at the bruises on my legs, the ones I got the night I fell over boxes trying to escape Reno in my room. "Exactly. And if Inez hadn't dropped clues about Graceland, you wouldn't have asked Nina to help. You guys didn't really know each other before, right?"

"I knew she has some weird hobbies," Andrew chuckles.

"And I knew he smells like a donkey after gym class," Nina adds, raising an eyebrow as if baiting him to say something else.

"Don't you see? Inez never tried to hurt me. She never tried to hurt any of us. She just . . . brought us together."

Nina's mouth curves up into a smile. "I didn't want to say it before because I was afraid I would upset you, but I haven't had this much fun in a *long* time."

"Me neither," Andrew says with a sheepish grin. "I mean, I don't wanna be a Ghostbuster or anything, but I had fun."

"What about all the soccer you missed?" I ask, feeling bad.

He stands up and bounces on the balls of his feet. "Everyone needs a break sometimes. When I go back, I'll tear things up. I'll have my position back in no time."

I hope that's true. Reaching into the side pocket of my backpack, I pull out my half-empty water bottle and lift it into the air. "To Inez."

With a straight face, Andrew lifts his Gatorade bottle. Nina searches her backpack frantically, finally coming up with an open bag of Goldfish. Lifting it in the air, she laughs loudly. More loudly than I've ever heard her laugh.

"To Inez."

40

LIFTING THE PASTEL OFF MY SKETCHPAD, I stare down at the bold outline I've just completed. The name *Inez Briggs* in clean, perfect strokes. Usually, I would fill in with different colors, but looking at these letters, I know the best choice is jet black, and only black. It will stand out best that way. All it needs now is to be shaded in and laminated, and then it's ready.

"Hey, Jonah—come here, buddy. Bring Reno."

Jonah looks at me skeptically, his hands pausing in midair over a mess of Lego people. "Are you going to do something to him?"

Once upon a time, I would have gladly tried to burn Reno. Not anymore. Not now that I understand why Inez needed him. "No. I don't want to hurt him. Swear." I hold up my pinky. "Actually, I want to show him something."

Jonah scoops Reno up off the floor and tucks him into his chest. Dodging a carpet full of spare Lego arms, legs, and heads, he makes his way toward me and looks down at the paper. "What is it?"

I smile and tap on the letters one at a time. "*I-N-E-Z.* That spells *Inez.* She's a friend of mine, a little girl who helped me a lot, and I want to thank her by making this."

"Why do you need Reno?" Jonah asks, popping a thumb in his mouth.

Moving Jonah's thumb from his lips, I give him a look. The one that says *You're too old to be sucking your thumb.* I know Mom and Dad won't tell him, but I've decided I'm okay with that. I'm done being angry because they aren't like other parents. They're different—complicated—and that's okay. Like it's okay for my new friends.

Andrew acts like soccer is his life, but it's really his friends.

Richie pretends his best feature is his stomach, but it's actually his brain.

Nina seems shy but talks more than Rachel when she's excited.

Cassidy fakes not needing help, but she just doesn't know how to ask for it.

And me? I act like I hate the adventure jar, but I secretly love it.

"You told me one time you thought ghosts were in this house. Remember?" I ask once Jonah's thumb is secured at his side.

"Yes."

"And do you still think that?" I've always suspected that Inez came to me because of my art, but that doesn't explain why Jonah heard her our first night here. Part of me wonders if he heard her because he wanted to.

Jonah looks out the window for a moment, then turns to face me. There's no trace of fear in his eyes this time. No worry. He shrugs. "I don't know. But it's not sad anymore."

It's not sad anymore. I really hope this is true. Snatching my sketchpad back off the floor, I hold it in front of him. "Can you ask Reno to look at this? I mean, I think my friend—Inez—probably really likes Reno. So if he thinks this picture is good, she will, too!"

Jonah drags Reno into a sitting position and props him up against the couch. The deep black orbs of his eyes stare down at the paper.

"Okay, let him have a good look. I need Reno's

stamp of approval before I show this to my friend, Inez." Waiting for Jonah's reaction, I hold my hands in my lap to keep them from shaking. Jonah doesn't understand how important this is to me. He might say the doll hates it, and then I'll have to start from scratch. But if I've learned anything since moving to Chicago, it's that I need to face my fears. Mean girls, ghosts, and terrifying ventriloquist dummies . . . I can't let them win. And today I'm starting with Reno.

A frigid blast of air shoots through the room, ruffling my hair. Jonah opens his mouth to say something, but I hold my hand up to stop him. If Inez is here and she wants to tell me something, I don't want anyone to get in her way. The crackling starts up, slowly simmering under my skin until I feel her full energy pulsing through me. The house seems to hum with it . . . an invisible, endless force.

"Thank you." Reno's mouth suddenly clicks out in an alarmingly high-pitched voice. I fly up off the couch, adrenaline pumping through me like a wildfire. I didn't see Jonah's lips move that time. *Like, not even a little!* Has he really gotten that good at ventriloquism?

Jonah fumbles Reno, nearly dropping him on the floor. He holds the doll at arm's length and stares at it, his face a mixture of shock and happiness.

"Wow! Did you hear that, Tessa? Reno talked for real!" he screeches excitedly, and then races out of the room, probably to tell Dad.

I sit paralyzed.

What just happened?

I gasp as the only possibility, no matter how crazy, worms its way into my brain. The room looks empty, but I know with one hundred percent certainty that it isn't. No wonder the voice sounded so strange and his lips didn't move. It wasn't Jonah who did that. It was Inez.

Smiling, I begin to color in the letters of her name. With any luck, she's watching . . . and happy.

41

THE GATES OF GRACELAND CEMETERY LOOK different to me today. Less foreboding and more welcoming. I can't say I'm thrilled about walking through the gravestones, or passing those horrible mausoleums by myself, but I am happy about seeing Inez again. I have something for her.

I press the buzzer on the front office for the second time in the past week. The door clicks open and I walk into the lobby. I don't need a plot map this time; I remember how to get to Inez's box. I need information.

"Oh, hello again! Here to research some more?" The same woman greets me today. This time she has a pair of reading glasses perched on the bridge of her nose.

Research? I guess you could call it that. I've been worrying about something ever since I left Graceland the first time.

"Yes, thank you. I just had a question before I go back out there."

"Shoot," she says with a smile. She's in a better mood. Probably because there isn't a raging typhoon outside today.

It's time to test Cass's theory. "You said there are rumors about Inez's statue. That it disappears during electrical storms."

She chuckles and raises one finely plucked eyebrow. "Yes. I hope I set a good atmosphere for you and your friends last time."

Atmosphere? Was she *trying* to freak us out and give me a heart attack?

"There have been rumors that the statue disappears, yes. But our grounds keepers have an explanation for that."

Aha. I hold my breath, waiting for her to continue. Hoping she'll confirm what Cassidy said and ease my fears that the last time I was here, Inez was angry and restless enough to try to keep me.

"Oh, you poor dear! You look terrified!" The woman laughs, garnering the attention of the other women working at desks behind her. "It's just fogged up! When the weather changes abruptly, the air temperature makes the inside of the glass box fog up with condensation, and boom! You have a ghostly missing statue."

"Fogged up," I repeat. Cassidy was right. "Wow. So simple."

"It usually is, honey." She smiles warmly and I turn to leave. Everything is still exactly how it was when Andrew, Nina, and I originally came here. The chairs, the pictures, the brochures. But now the puzzle is complete.

The woman glances at my hands and her eyes trail back up to mine. "Interesting doll."

I hold Reno up higher and straighten the red bow tie around his neck. "Thanks. He's . . . ahhh . . . a friend."

She waggles one eyebrow as if seventh graders shouldn't be playing with dolls, but I don't care. I'm visiting Inez today, and if she likes Reno, I'm going to make sure she gets to see him. She was only six years old when she died—the perfect age for enjoying a ventriloquist dummy. It's not fair that she didn't get a chance to.

I head out the door and make my way toward Inez. A beautiful autumn sunshine is beating down on my neck and warming it. Leaves drift lazily down to my feet, and I notice how bare the tree branches are getting. In three weeks it will be Halloween, and everyone will be dressed up, running door-to-door with sacks of candy. When we first moved here, I would've said trick-or-treating is out of the question. That it's too dangerous in a city this big. But now I think it could be fun. Shady Street is safe and well-lit, and mom says our neighbors seem nice. Plus there are a few big houses with really cool decorations in their lawn. If they have giant stashes of candy, then this could be one of the best Halloweens I've ever had. Especially if I can spend it with Andrew, Nina, and Richie.

The glass box appears just around the bend, and my breath catches in my throat. There she is. The little girl no one understands. The girl everyone would prefer to leave shrouded in mystery just because it's a better ghost story.

Taking a few more steps, I home in on her sculpted face. Seeing her petite features again is really a rush. She's so pretty. So young, too. Younger than me, but not all that different. She was missing her home. Her *place.* Just. Like. Me.

A strong, unseasonably warm breeze picks up, lifting my hair off my shoulders and whipping it into my face. It isn't scary like the time we got stuck in here and the thunderstorm came through. Instead, it's comforting.

"I know you didn't haunt me just because you wanted your story and your name known," I say, knowing full well that if anyone saw me carrying on a conversation with a statue, they'd think I'm a crazy person. I don't care. My parents have never cared what others think about their quirky ways, and maybe part of me doesn't, either.

Smiling, I put the palm of my hand against the glass that separates us and say a silent "Thank you." The truth was so much simpler than I ever made it. Inez haunting me was never *just* about setting her story straight. It was about helping me in the only way she could. By giving me her mystery to figure out, she also gave me friends.

Propping Reno up against the base of her box, I slide my messenger bag off my shoulder and set it on the ground. Reaching in, my fingers find what they're looking for—the eight-by-ten-inch laminated sheet of paper. I pull it out and then go for the duct tape I snagged from the pantry.

"You helped me find Nina, Andrew, and Richie, and I owe you. I'm going to fix this for you, Inez," I whisper. The trees above me rattle and I wonder if she's listening. If she's watching.

I hope so.

Placing the paper over the name *Inez Clarke* etched into the plaque at the base of the statue, I make sure it's straight before taping it on. I don't know how long it will stay or if the winter snowstorms will tear it down, but I'll always come back and fix it. I'll make sure people know.

INEZ BRIGGS
SEPTEMBER 20, 1873
AUGUST 1, 1880

I might not be able to change the fact that Inez had to move to a new house without her mother and father. Or that her glass box is in all the ghost books. But I can at least keep the correct name on her gravestone. After all she went through to reach me, and the friends I've made because of her story, I owe her at least that much.

EPILOGUE

"DON'T GET YOUR ZOMBIE SKIN ON IT! YOU'RE going to smudge it, dummy!" Nina shoves Andrew and he nearly falls off his chair, raining flecks of dried green paint onto the carpet. Richie laughs and crams another handful of popcorn in his mouth. I think he's secretly happy that Nina is finally fighting with someone other than him.

I look up from the image on my paper and smile. Today is filled with firsts. My first time drawing a person. My first time letting people watch me draw. My first time sharing my art with friends. It felt scary at first, but now I'm happy. So happy it hurts.

It's also my first time celebrating Halloween anywhere but Florida. I wasn't sure how things would go, but when Andrew, Nina, and Richie showed up wearing costumes even though we're almost teenagers, I knew the night was going to rock. We might not have done as much actual trick-or-treating as my little brother did, but we've definitely had fun.

"Wow! Tessa, it looks amazing so far!" Andrew says, leaning closer. He catches Nina giving him a dirty look, then sighs and slides his elbow safely away. "I can't believe you came up with this just based on the sculpture."

Looking down, I can't help but feel proud. Even without having an actual picture of what Inez looked like, I think my drawing is pretty accurate. Long rumpled-up hair—as Andrew would say—with a ribbon in it. Kind eyes, and a sweet little-girl smile. "Thanks."

Nina kicks her legs out to untangle the bottom of her long black dress. A pair of Nike sneakers peeks out from the bottom of the fabric. When she first showed up, I thought she was a witch, but I should have known better. A witch is too boring—too *generic*—for Nina. Apparently, she's something called a spiritualist. Guess a long time ago they used to tell people they could communicate with the dead. Even though she still kinda looks like a witch to me, the whole spiritualist thing makes way more sense for a girl who's obsessed with ghosts.

I gesture to her shoes. "Okay. I get the Ouija board you're carrying, but what's up with the Nikes?"

Nina quickly tucks the shoes back under her skirt. "Hey, don't judge my footwear! According to my research, people in the eighteen hundreds had *very* uncomfortable shoes."

I burst out laughing. Nina purses her lips as if she's not going to laugh, then gives in and starts cackling. It's been nice to watch her finally come out of her shell. I hardly ever see her fishbowl eyes anymore, and she talks more than she used to. Way more. In fact, this whole night was her idea!

"So the people at Graceland are definitely going to hang it?" she asks, pointing to my drawing. "Where?"

"Yup. It's going to be in the lobby. Right next to the front desk." I add the slightest bit of pink to Inez's cheeks. Not a lot, just enough to bring her skin to life.

It's been three weeks since I started hanging the correct name on Inez Briggs's gravestone. And even though I thought I was being sneaky about it, it didn't take the cemetery very long to figure out what I was up to. After I'd started passing through the gates every few days with my stash of signs and tape, they finally caught up with me and asked if I was responsible for the new signage on Inez's grave.

Thankfully, I told them the truth, or none of these amazing things would be happening. I wouldn't have been on the cover of the *Chicago Sun-Times* with Andrew and Nina, talking about Inez's story. The *real* story. I wouldn't have made more friends in this new place than I know what to do with. And I definitely wouldn't be drawing a picture of Inez for the front office at Graceland. They're going to hang it in honor of her. As suspected, the death certificate I found *is* real, and very special. Nina was right all along; it was the missing piece. Mom and Dad gave it to the cemetery for their files, which is fine by me because even though I'm not scared of Inez anymore, death certificates are spooky with a capital *S*.

Maybe from now on Inez won't just be remembered in ghost books, or on Halloween. Maybe she'll be remembered the way she should be: as a brave little girl.

"It's beautiful, honey. Just beautiful. Maybe when it's finished we could look into getting your art carried in a few other places around here?" Mom asks. She bends down to get a closer look, accidentally draping her vampire cape over my head.

Uncovering myself, I laugh at the fake fangs hanging from her mouth. Mom and Dad dress up every year. Doesn't matter if we have plans or if they're just handing out candy; they love Halloween. "I'm not good enough yet, Mom. Your art should come first, anyway."

Mom plants a kiss on the top of my head. "We're a team, Tessa. My art, your art, it doesn't matter. What matters is that you're doing what you love!"

Dad grins as he scrapes a pocketknife along the small, rectangular chunk of rosin in his hand. Rosin is a strange thing. It looks like gel and makes the bow slide across the violin strings in just the right way. It makes the music sound better.

Like my family, I think. We might be a little weird, but we're happy.

Mom wraps an arm around Dad's shaggy shoulders, rumpling his wolf suit at the neckline just enough that I can see a Hawaiian-print shirt under.

"And how's my violin-playing Wolfman? Not many of those in the world! Can I have an autograph?" She kisses him on his furry cheek and I look away. I'm glad they aren't fighting like Cassidy's parents, but honestly . . . that's gross.

"Wolfman give autograph!" Dad bares his teeth like a dog, snatches a pen from the counter, and starts scrawling on Mom's arm before she can scamper away. Grinning, she grabs a pen of her own and wields it like a sword in front of her. Both of them dissolve into laughter.

I reach down and run the pad of my index finger over the glass screen of my new phone, smiling. It suddenly illuminates, displaying my father's name and picture. Looking up, I meet his eyes. He winks and holds up his phone. Why is he calling me from ten feet away?

"Hello?" I whisper into my phone.

"Are you happy, Tessa?" he asks, a familiar joy in his voice.

Yes, I'm happy. Right now, I think I might be the happiest girl in Chicago. But it isn't just about the phone. It's *everything.* I nod.

"Good. We love you, Tess. So much." His voice drifts through my phone and I clutch it more tightly. "Now go. Enjoy your friends. Your mother and I are going to go make sure Jonah is actually asleep and not playing around."

The line goes dead and I set my phone on the table. Andrew winks at me, and the smile that stretches across his painted face is electric. Brilliant. *Perfect.* It's good enough that I try to memorize it like I would a subject I'm planning to draw. I don't know if he'll keep liking me, or if I'll keep liking him, but the thought gives me butterflies and I hope the answer is yes.

I slide a hand up to the locket around my neck and soak in the feeling fluttering around in my chest.

It's a good one. A safe and happy one. Inez hasn't haunted me since I hung her name that very first day. The cold breeze has disappeared from our hallways. The crying and the doorknob rattling have stopped and the picture in the hallway stays bright.

"Okay, get together! I don't have any pictures of you guys and it's time to change that!" I motion to Andrew, Richie, and Nina to stand side by side and center them perfectly on the screen of my phone camera. Snapping the photo, I laugh at the side-eye Nina is giving Richie. Classic. Maybe next time we do this, Cassidy will be with us. I hope so, because now that I know she doesn't hate me, I want a chance to hear her hyena laugh and her travel stories. I want to know her.

I open Rachel's latest text message and send her the picture I just took. She's been asking for days now to see what everyone looks like, but I didn't have anything to send her. Now I have a zombie, a spiritualist, and . . . what was Richie again? Oh, yeah, a hot dog. Ha! My eyes drift to the corner where his abandoned costume is lying in a heap, and I giggle. I hope Rachel can come here soon, because she'll love these guys and they'll love her. I just know it.

Setting down my phone, I kick my feet up onto the table and enjoy the chaos. Richie dangling a fake spider in Nina's face, Andrew laughing so hard he's about to fall off his chair . . . *again* . . . and Reno, propped in the corner with a tiny fake mustache stuck to his face. It was hard giving up Rachel. Moving here. Leaving behind everything I love. But I realize now that I'll grow to love Chicago just as much. My friends are cool. My neighborhood is amazing. Even Shady Street isn't half bad anymore! If it's possible to owe a ghost, I totally do.

Thanks, Inez. For *everything.*

ACKNOWLEDGMENTS

Thank you for reading Tessa's story! Although I wrote *The Peculiar Incident on Shady Street,* it would not be in your hands right now without the support of so many incredible people. Below are those incredible people; I hope you'll take a moment out of your day to read about them and how they helped bring Tessa's journey to the shelves.

Thank you to my agent, Kathleen Rushall, for believing in *Peculiar Incident* and championing it from the very first draft I dropped in your inbox. Your support and keen editorial eye have helped to make my little ghost story a reality, and for that I'm forever grateful.

A huge thank-you goes out to my amazing editor, Amy Cloud. Your insight, encouragement, and patience have been beyond inspiring. I'm grateful for the countless hours you spent reading and rereading this novel, the brilliant edits you provided, and the life you breathed into Tessa's story throughout this process. Watching *Peculiar Incident* transform from a mass of jumbled words that my brain spit out to a fully formed novel has been a dream come true, and I'm grateful for the opportunity to work with you on it.

To the entire publishing team at Aladdin/S&S—THANK YOU! From the moment I signed my contract for this book, I've experienced nothing but pride. Pride because every step of this process has been handled with passion and attention to detail. Thank you to publisher Mara Anastas, to deputy publisher Mary Marotta, to art director Jessica Handelman, and to managing editor Chelsea Morgan. Your support and hard work on this book mean the world to me.

Hugs, virtual cupcakes, and *all* the smiley emoji faces go out to my amazing group of writerly friends, who not only supported me throughout the drafting process for this novel, but inspire me with their talent every single day. Thank you to Jessica Lawson, Jenna Lehne, Jess Keating, Becky Wallace, Jenni Walsh, Marci Curtis, Lynne Matson, and Tracey Neithercott. I'm forever grateful to know (and love) you ladies.

Thank you to the talented and fabulous artists who sent me fan art inspired by *Peculiar Incident*—Gabrielle Jones and Jessica Bates. You two are the original members of Tessa's Art Squad, and I could not be more honored to showcase some of your work on my website!

And to my family . . .

I owe you the biggest thanks of all. I owe you not only for giving me the time and space to dive into this world when I needed it, but also for believing in me.

Rob, Ben, and Ella—you three are my biggest, best, and most wonderful journey. You inspire me to be a better mother and writer every day with your kindness, empathy, intelligence, and beauty. There would be no books without you. I love you all to the moon and back.

John—if I could press a button and show teenage Lindsay how we turned out, I'd do it in a heartbeat. Thank you for being my laugh when I need one, for going on ghost tours with me on date nights, for swapping dinners with me when I hate mine, and for simply being you. There would be no books without you, either. I love you.

Mom and Dad—you let me bring home the stray animals, put on the "performances," write the poems, sing the songs, and read the books. You helped me become exactly who I needed to be: a writer. Thank you!

Bob, Sue, and Dave—in-laws might get a bad rap, but I seriously lucked out with you guys. Your support and encouragement on this book—on *every* book—mean a lot to me. Thank you!

ABOUT THE AUTHOR

Lindsay Currie lives in Chicago with one incredibly patient hubby, three amazing kids, and a 160-pound lapdog named Sam. She's fond of tea, Halloween, Disney World, and things that go bump in the night.